The Citizen Reader

Publisher's Note

The Citizen Reader by H. O. Arnold-Forster was originally written in the late 19th century as an educational book for British schoolchildren. It reflects the values, beliefs, and perspectives of its time, particularly regarding government, empire, and national identity. While much of the book provides valuable insights into civic duty, governance, and history, some passages express outdated and unfortunate views on race and colonialism that do not align with modern understanding.

These aspects serve as a reminder of how perspectives on society and culture have evolved. Rather than dismissing the work entirely, we encourage readers to approach it with a critical eye—appreciating its useful lessons while recognizing its historical limitations. Thoughtful engagement with historical texts allows us to learn both from their strengths and their shortcomings.

This edition published 2025
by Living Book Press

Copyright © Living Book Press, 2025

ISBN: 978-1-76153-834-6 (hardcover)
        978-1-76153-807-0 (softcover)

First published in 1885.

All rights reserved. No part of this publication may be reproduced, stored in a retrieval system, or transmitted in any other form or means – electronic, mechanical, photocopying, recording or otherwise, without the prior permission of the copyright owner and the publisher or as provided by Australian law.

A catalogue record for this book is available from the National Library of Australia

The Citizen Reader

by

H. O. ARNOLD FORSTER

MAP OF THE WORLD
(British Possessions Coloured Red)

Contents

LA·BELLE
SAUVAGE

PREFACE.

THIS "Citizen Reader" seems to me a successful attempt to fill a gap in school books which I am surprised has not been filled before. There is no doubt that the enormous majority of school children will have public as well as private duties to perform—the boys, in most cases, by direct action, and the girls by indirect but powerful influence. They will be called upon not only to lead an upright life and to do what they rightly can to help those who are bound to them by family ties, but it will also be their duty to serve their country as patriotic citizens; and the fulfilment of this duty will be greatly aided by some knowledge of the institutions of their country.

The object of this book is to describe, in language which a child can understand, the principles and purpose of our institutions, the machinery of our administration, and also to tell children what ought to be the principles which should actuate them as patriotic citizens.

The last aim is, without doubt, a difficult one. It is not easy to fulfil it without affronting prejudices or, indeed, honest convictions. But I think any unbiased reader will admit that there is little, if anything, in this book which will not be accepted by men of all creeds and parties.

It is well known that our English educational system is almost alone in the refusal of Government either to prescribe or to authorise school books. There is much to be said for and against this course, but, on the other hand, the Education Code, by permitting the use of a variety of Readers in our elementary schools, gives ample opportunity for the introduction of works such as this. Already much has been done by the issue of specially prepared books to instruct children with regard to history, science, and other branches of learning. Why should not a similar effort be made to instruct them in the duties of citizenship? I need not dwell upon what must be apparent to all, namely, that there is special fitness in the appearance of a book of this kind at a time when we have just added millions to the citizens who have the right of electing representatives.

I can, therefore, commend the "Citizen Reader" to the consideration of those who are interested in education, as a fair and, in my opinion, not unsuccessful attempt to supply a deficiency which has remained too long unfilled.

W. E. FORSTER.

London, 1885.

NOTE TO SEVENTH EDITION:

SOME fresh illustrations have been inserted in the present edition, and the statistics of population corrected up to date, Jan. 1887.

NOTE TO EIGHTH EDITION:

FOUR pages of new matter have been added in this edition to the chapter on Taxation.

NOTE TO TENTH EDITION:

THE present edition contains a considerable number of fresh illustrations prepared especially for this work.

NOTE TO FOURTEENTH EDITION:

THE institution of County Councils under the Act of 1888 has made it necessary to insert a few pages explaining the nature and functions of these important bodies.

INTRODUCTION

THIS work is intended to instruct boys and girls in our elementary schools with regard to their rights, duties, and privileges as British citizens. It contains an account, in simple and popular language, of the principles of the legislative and administrative arrangements of the country, explains the meaning and value of our chief popular liberties, and describes the duties owed by British citizens to their country, their countrymen, and themselves.

"The life of a people grows; it is knit together and yet expanded, in joy and sorrow, in thought and action. It absorbs the thought of other nations into its own forms, and gives back the thought as new wealth to the world. It is a power and an organ in the great body of the nations. But there may come a check, an arrest; memories may be stifled, and love may be faint for the lack of them; or memories may shrink into withered relics—the soul of a people—whereby they know themselves to be one, may seem to be dying for want of common action. But who shall say, 'The fountain of their life is dried up; they shall forever cease to be a nation'? Who shall say it? Not he who feels the life of his people stirring within his own. Shall he say, 'That way events are wending; I will not resist'? His very soul is resistance and is as a seed of fire that may enkindle the souls of multitudes and make a new pathway for events."

GEORGE ELIOT

CHAPTER I.

WHAT IS MEANT BY BEING A GOOD CITIZEN

"I am a citizen of no mean city."

I.
The Country We Belong To.

1. THE words taken as the motto of this chapter were used by St. Paul, and the city of which he spoke was Tarsus, in Asia Minor.

2. The words which he uttered may certainly be repeated by every one of us; and if St. Paul was proud of being a citizen of Tarsus, we who live in England or in any part of the great British Empire may indeed say with pride that we, too, are "citizens of no mean country."

3. Look at the map at the beginning of this book, and think what is meant by all those red patches which you will see dotted over every part of it.

4. They mean that, in every part of the world so marked, there are countrymen of ours living and working; that in every continent and in every climate there are men and women who read the same English Bible that we read, who enjoy the same great books that we enjoy—Shakespeare, Milton, Burns; men and women who look back to the same history that we look back to, who speak our language, who use our laws, and who are ready to share our dangers and to rejoice in our good fortune.

5. Some of you, perhaps, have friends across the sea, and in that way, you may have learnt to understand that there are Englishmen

far away from England who live lives like ours at home. And all of you ought to remember that the great nation to which you belong, and of which I hope you are all proud, is far bigger than the two little islands which make up the kingdom of Great Britain and Ireland, and that it extends everywhere where the English language is spoken by men who live under English law and under the English flag.

Why We Are Proud of Our Country.

6. I said that I hoped you were all proud of your country, but I trust you did not think that I wished you to be proud of it only because it was big. That would be a great mistake. It would be just as sensible to say that a man was a good man simply because he was a big one, as to say that a country was to be admired because it covered a great many square miles. You know that what makes a man great and honourable is what he does and not what he looks like.

7. Some of the weakest and smallest men have yet been the noblest and the most useful. St. Paul himself, whose words we read just now, was a man who had no great strength; he tells us, indeed, that he was "in bodily presence weak, and in speech contemptible." It is the spirit and mind of a man that give him his power; and so it is with England or with any other country: it will be truly great and honourable only if it does things which in themselves are honourable and worthy. If England does wrong, and uses its power to injure others unjustly, then, however big and strong the country may be, however victorious in war, however prosperous in peace, there will be no reason to be proud of it.

England Is What We Make It.

8. But I have been talking to you about England doing right and England doing wrong, and I think it is time you should ask me what I mean by England and how it is that I can speak about a great country as if I were speaking of a man or a woman.

9. When we speak of a country doing right and wrong, we mean that the people who live in it, and who decide how it shall be governed, have chosen the good way or the bad way. Who is it, then, that makes England do right or wrong? Who is it that makes it a country to be proud of or a country to be ashamed of? Think for yourselves a moment, and you will see that it is you and I, and all of us who take any part in governing the country, who decide the matter. And remember that all of you who grow up to be men will have votes, and will help to send members to Parliament, so that you will really and truly help to govern the country.[1]

10. But giving votes for members of Parliament is not by any means the only way in which you will be able to make a difference. Nor is it the men only who help or harm the country. The women are just as much bound to think of the part they ought to play in making England great and happy as the men. If they care about doing it, there will always be plenty of ways in which they can set to work.

11. You will see now that it is no good talking about the greatness of the country or pretending to be proud of it unless we who live in the country really do something to make it great, and of which we, and those who come after us, have a right to be proud.

II.
How to Become a Good Citizen

1   At the time *The Citizen Reader* was written, voting rights were generally restricted to men in many countries. Women's suffrage movements around the world fought for equal voting rights, leading to significant changes in the 20th century. Below are key dates when women gained the right to vote in various countries:
New Zealand – 1893 (first self-governing country to grant women voting rights)
Australia – 1902 (excluding Indigenous women in some states until 1962)
United Kingdom – 1918 (for women over 30); 1928 (equal voting rights with men at 21)
Canada – 1917–1918 (gradual; full voting rights for Indigenous women in 1960)
United States – 1920 (19th Amendment)
South Africa – 1930 (for white women; full voting rights for all women in 1994)

1. I am going to try in this book to explain to you what are the ways in which this country is governed, and to show you how our laws are made, and why we should obey them, to point out the best ways in which you can serve the country, and how you can become really good and useful citizens.

2. It is perhaps hard to understand at first how there can be any difference between being a good citizen and being a good man or woman. And in one sense, it is true, there is no difference; for a bad man or a bad woman will never be a really good citizen. But while I want you not to forget this, I want you to give your special attention to those things which people have to do for the sake of others, quite apart from their own family and friends, in order that the country may be wisely and justly governed, and may be respected and honoured by foreign nations.

Private Duties

3. You will easily see what I mean if I give you an example. Suppose you or I were to be living, like Robinson Crusoe, alone on an island. Although we were quite alone, we should still be just as much bound to try and do right, as far as we were able, as if we lived in a busy town.

4. We should not be cruel to animals; we should try and keep our body in health, so that our mind might be clear and healthy too; and you may be sure there are other ways also in which we should find opportunities of choosing the right or the wrong way. But if we were asked to do the duties of a good citizen, I certainly think we should be puzzled about how to set about it.

5. And so, too, in our own families, there are hundreds of ways in which we may do our duty or avoid doing it. But whether we do it or not will depend upon how we have been taught by our parents, how much we love those who are near to us, and will have very little to do with our duties as citizens.

6. But when we come to live in a great and busy country like this,

where there are millions of people all working in different ways and for different ends, when we have to act in such a way that we shall do no injustice to others nor suffer injustice ourselves, then we must directly begin to think about what I will call public duty, and we must make up our minds how we should behave so that not only we in our own homes shall be happy and prosperous, but that all our fellow countrymen, rich and poor, high and low, may be happy and prosperous too. To learn how to do this is to learn how to become a good citizen.

The Common Rule

7. But though the things we may have to do as citizens are different from what we have to do as private people among our own family and friends, there is no difference in the rules which ought to guide us in the one case and in the other, and that is why it is worthwhile to begin thinking about these questions while we are young and still at school.

8. The very same lessons of kindness, truth, honour, and obedience which you learn at home from your parents, at school from your teachers, and in church or chapel from your clergymen, ministers, and priests, have to be remembered and acted upon when you grow up, and become voters, or taxpayers, soldiers, sailors, or jurymen; in fact, in all the things which you may ever have to do for the good of your country and the welfare of your countrymen.

9. Just as at home it is sometimes your duty to deny yourself some amusement or advantage for the sake of your mother and sisters or friends, or, again, as you may possibly have to suffer some pain or inconvenience for their good; so it often becomes the duty of men and women, when they grow up, to deny themselves advantages, to suffer loss or pain, not that their own friends and relations among whom they live may be the better, but that all the people of this country may gain, that England may do what is just and right—that England may help, and not injure, those who live in foreign countries.

How Lancashire Did Its Duty

10. I will give you one or two examples of men and women doing their duty in this way as citizens, which will show you what I mean better than I can explain it to you. Not very long ago, in the year 1861, a great war broke out across the Atlantic, in the United States of America. It was one of those terrible wars which are called "civil wars," that is to say, those who fought on either side belonged to the same nation and were really one people.

11. The war began about a dispute between the States in the North and the States in the South as to their exact rights of interfering with each other in the making of laws. But before long, it became quite clear that the real question which both sides were determined to settle was a very different one—it was the question of whether there should be any more slaves in the United States or not.

12. The Northern States had given up slavery themselves, and they were determined that it should come to an end in the South too. The "Southerners," who employed the slaves to cultivate their cotton plantations, were equally determined not to give up their right to buy and sell the negroes and to make them work for them for nothing. But you will perhaps ask what all this has to do with English citizens and their duties. I am coming to that, and when I have told you a little more, I think you will see that it has a great deal to do with it.

13. I said that the "Southerners" required their slaves to cultivate the cotton for them. The cotton, as you know, is a plant from the pod of which is taken the material which is spun into calico to make shirts and handkerchiefs, and a hundred other things which we use every day.

14. At the time of the war in the United States, nearly all the cotton grown in the South was sent to Lancashire and there spun and woven in the mills by English factory hands. No less than 800,000 people were employed in the various mills. But before the war had been going on long, it became clear that the cotton would be prevented from reaching Liverpool, for in order to conquer the Southern States, the Northern

States ordered their ships to stop all vessels carrying cotton from the Southern harbours. What is called a blockade was declared, and the different ports were soon really blocked.

15. This all happened thousands of miles away, but its effect was very soon felt near home. In Lancashire, the supply of cotton ran short, the mills were compelled to stop running, and the thousands of people who were employed in them were thrown out of work. To be out of work was to be out of wages, and before long, many were actually starving, while very many more were supported by charity only. The distress increased even faster than the means of relief, and although nearly three million pounds were given by the Government, or subscribed by friends of the sufferers, the greatest misery prevailed.

16. It was plain to everybody that if the South were to be victorious, or if the North were made to give up the blockade, the cotton would soon begin to pour into Liverpool again, and there were many people in England at the time who did all they could to help the South and to try and make Parliament take their part.

17. But in spite of their suffering, the working men of Lancashire would never consent to help the cause of slavery. They knew that across the Atlantic the Northerners were fighting in the cause of freedom and justice against the bullets of the enemy. They were determined that they, at least, would not make the battle harder for the friends of right, and that, at any rate, as far as they were concerned, our country should do its duty, even though they had to suffer for it.

18. And so, as good citizens, they put into practice the rule of right which they had learnt to be a just one in their own families and their own business, and they stood up all through the war for the cause of liberty. Lancashire would not join in the cry against the North, and thus the Government were able to keep up their friendship with the United States and avoid the terrible consequences of a great war. This is an instance of how we can do our duty as citizens in big things, but

I could give you plenty of examples of how needful it is to do it in small things too.

III.
How We Can Help the Country

1. Every time one of us is courteous and civil to a foreigner, he is doing his part as a good citizen, for he is helping to make his country liked and respected abroad. Every time a man walks to the polling place and gives his vote honestly for a member of Parliament, he is doing his part as a good citizen in helping to make the Government of the country honest and fair.

2. Every time a mother sends her child to school, she is doing her duty as a good citizen, for the law says that all children must be educated, and it is the part of a good citizen to obey the law. And lastly, every boy or girl who goes to school willingly and cheerfully is doing his or her duty as a good citizen, for of course it would be no good at all for the law to send children to school if the children themselves wasted their time and neglected their work when they got there.

3. So you will see that there are many ways, both great and small, in which we may all of us show that we are good citizens and are willing to serve our country.

4. And lastly, there is one other and most important way in which we may help our country, help our neighbours, and help ourselves, and that is to be careful in our own lives to live honestly and well, for no amount of good laws, no great victories, and no great riches will make a country great if the people who live in it do not try themselves to be true and just in all their dealings, remembering that to rule oneself is the first step to being able to rule others.

Two Ways of Doing Our Duty

5. These and all the other things which I shall have to mention to you are matters with which every one of you may at some time or another have to do when you grow up. Some of them, indeed, you have a good deal to do with now.

6. There will always be two ways of doing your duty as good citizens. The one way is to do it because you are obliged, and because you cannot help it. The other, and the better way, is to do it because you understand it, and because you feel that in doing it well you are helping at the same time your country, your countrymen, and yourself. We very often have to do things during our lives of which we do not understand the reasons, but the more clearly we understand the work we have to do, depend upon it, the better the work will be done.

7. And now I must come to the real lessons I want you to learn in order that you may become good and useful citizens. There are some rules we must all learn and some things we must all be able to do; but the most important thing of all is to learn what we have to learn and to do what we have to do in the proper spirit.

8. And that is why, before I tell you anything about laws and law-making, and voting, and other very important matters, I am going to give up a chapter to explaining to you what is meant by *Patriotism*, because if you understand that, you will see also how in all that we do as citizens we can serve our country as well as ourselves.

CHAPTER II.

PATRIOTISM

"Not once nor twice in our rough island story
The path of duty was the way to glory." – *Tennyson*

IV.
What the Word Means

1. PATRIOTISM comes from the Latin word *Patria*[2], and means love of one's country or of one's fatherland. The words patriotism and patriotic are often misused and misunderstood, but when properly and truly understood, they describe a great and worthy feeling, which ought to fill the mind of every man and woman. It is right that every man and woman should love the country in which they live, and on whose good fortune their own happiness depends. You all know that the first love which we have is for our own family and our own friends: we wish them to succeed, and we wish them to be happy; nay, more, we try to make them so.

2. And what is true of the small circle of our friends and relations is true also of the larger circles into which we are brought as we grow older. Boys and girls, when they go to school, are nearly always proud of their school and are anxious for its credit and good name. A boy wishes his own school to be the best at cricket, at football, at examinations, in winning scholarships, in work, and in play; and you will see just the same thing among grown-up people: each county,

---

2   *Pater* means father; *Patria*, fatherland.

each regiment, each district will be proud of its own history and anxious to add to its own good fame.

3. If it be rightly understood and rightly acted upon, this feeling is a very good and a very helpful one, for a man who tries to do better than his neighbour must needs do well himself. A schoolboy who tries to keep up the credit of his school, a soldier who longs to add to the fame of his regiment, will always feel that much is expected of him by others, and as a rule, a boy or a man will do more the more you expect of him.

4. And so it is with patriotism and the love of country: those who really love their country and are truly proud of its great history will be particularly careful not to do anything by which it may be dishonoured. On the other hand, they will always try with all their power to place their country before all others in every right and noble work, and so it comes about that they will often give up their lives and their fortunes, not that their own immediate friends and families may be the gainers, but in order that their country may be saved from danger, and that others may think well of it.

5. There are many instances in our long history in which country-men of ours have given up life and wealth for their country, and we who are alive now owe much to what they have suffered and sacrificed.

The True Patriot

6. Every British citizen ought to remember one very important thing about the patriotism which has made our country what it is. Those who love their country best are content to serve it without the hope of immediate reward or even the encouragement of praise.

7. Sometimes it may be that the very act which is performed for the sake of England is done far away from any friendly eye, with no certainty that friends at home will ever even know of it, and yet, for the sake of duty and love of country, the deed will be done.

The Magazine at Delhi

8. There is a story of a brave action, done during the great mutiny in India, which will show you very clearly what I mean. It was at the time when the Sepoys, or native soldiers, in a great part of India had risen against the English. In many places, all the white people had been killed; in others, they had been shut up and besieged in different forts and towns. There were very few English soldiers ready, and it seemed at one time as if every Englishman would be killed or driven out of India.

9. The great city of Delhi, in the north of India, was surrounded by the Sepoys, and had they taken it, the danger would at once have increased tenfold, for at Delhi was the great magazine in which were kept the gunpowder, the arms, and the stores which the English Government had provided for the use of the army. If once the Sepoys had got possession of the powder and arms, they would doubtless have been able to beat our small armies and to gain a complete victory.

10. But into the magazine at Delhi the Sepoys never got, for in it were a handful of English soldiers who were determined that, if the sacrifice of their lives could prevent it, the danger to their fellow-countrymen should not be increased. The enemy surrounded the magazine. Lieutenant Willoughby and his brave comrades knew well that to defend it was impossible, but they were determined that it should not be taken.

11. A train of gunpowder was laid down to the magazine, and as the enemy began to swarm over the walls, Willoughby gave the signal to light the match. "A roar followed as if the earth were splitting asunder, and while all Delhi, from the bank of the Jumna to the Cashmere Gate, shook and trembled, the mighty magazine exploded, and for a time a dark cloud overhung the palace and the city. Hundreds of the mutineers were blown into the air, but none of the brave defenders escaped without injury.

12. "Conductor Scully was so dreadfully wounded that for him

escape was impossible. Willoughby and Forrest succeeded in reaching the Cashmere Gate. The latter escaped, and the former was murdered on the road to Meerut; but Buckley and another reached headquarters in safety."

13. Such is the story of the Magazine of Delhi. What I want you to notice in it is that these men, who thus risked their lives for their country, did so far away from the eye of friends and without any of the encouragement which cheers those who do their duty in the sight of friends, and with the hope of reward.

V.

The Story of Columbus, and Its Lesson

1. Sometimes men and women may act in what they believe the best way for their country, even though at the time the wisdom and usefulness of what they are doing is not seen by those among whom they live, and their only reward at the time is hatred and mistrust. Not till long after is the good work they have done seen and understood by their countrymen.

2. Some of you will perhaps remember the story of Columbus, the great discoverer of America. What a difference to the world Columbus's discovery has made, it is impossible to exaggerate. Yet at the time, neither was the importance of his work understood by his countrymen, nor did he himself receive the honour and encouragement which his bravery and perseverance deserved. The story of Columbus and his adventures is a very sad one.

3. Four times did Columbus cross the Atlantic Ocean in the service of his country. The wonders of the New World were, for the first time, thrown open to those who lived in the Old World by his courage, his perseverance, and his skill. And what was the reward which he received during his lifetime for what he had done? Abandoned in his old age by King Ferdinand of Spain, to whose power

COLUMBUS DISCOVERING AMERICA.

and wealth he had added so much, he was refused not only generous treatment but even a fair hearing for his claims.

4. Suffering from a painful illness and worn out with the hardships of a life of danger and exposure, he tried in vain to gain the favour of the Court, if not for himself, at least for his son whom he was leaving behind him. The king was deaf to his appeal, and the greatest discoverer whom the world has ever known was left to die in sorrow and pain by those upon whom he had the greatest claim.

5. Let me give you an account of the death of Columbus by the great American writer, Washington Irving: -

"The cares and troubles of Columbus were drawing to a close. The momentary fire which had reanimated him was soon quenched by accumulating infirmities. His last voyage had shattered beyond repair a frame already worn and wasted by a life of hardships; and continual anxieties robbed him of that sweet repose so necessary to remit the weariness and debility of age.

6. "The cold ingratitude of his sovereign chilled his heart. The continued suspension of his honours, and the enmity and defamation experienced at every turn, seemed to throw a shadow over that glory which had been the great object of his ambition. This shadow, it is true, could be but of transient duration, but it is difficult for the most illustrious man to look beyond the present cloud which may obscure his fame, and anticipate its permanent lustre in the admiration of posterity."

7. We who have seen the cloud lifted, and who know that in our day Columbus's great work is fully understood, and that he himself is remembered not only by his own country of Spain but by all countries both in Europe and America as one of the noblest of the world's heroes, can feel true sorrow for the poor dying man, to whom the injustice of his lot was so clear, and who could not know what honour would be paid to his name when he was dead.

8. More than this, we may find in his story an example of how

the greatest services may be rendered to a nation or to the world by a man who, while he is doing his work, receives neither honour nor reward from his countrymen.

9. And in the history of this country, there always have been, and always will be, men who, like Columbus, have done some great work or found out some great truth which they have longed to put at the service of their countrymen. But the truth has been rejected, the service declined, and the man himself has had only suffering and disappointment in return for his efforts.

10. Not until his life was over did the seed which he had sown bear fruit, or the discovery which he had made fall into other hands better able to use it. But in the long run, the country has got the benefit of his work and has learnt to recognise a true patriot in the man who was despised and persecuted during his lifetime.

VI.
False Patriotism

1. There is, however, a false and a bad side to patriotism, which it is well to remember. You will sometimes hear people talk as if it was always right to support what is done by Englishmen in foreign countries, whether what they have done be right or wrong, only because those who have done it are English. This is wrong in itself, and can only lead us into troubles and difficulties; for it is plain that if Englishmen think it right to approve of or to overlook bad actions merely because it is an Englishman who has done them, it is equally likely that a Frenchman or a German will do the same thing when his own countrymen make mistakes or commit faults.

2. And so, all the world over, we should have great nations like England, Germany, and France supporting what they knew to be wrong for the sake of a false patriotism.

Be Just, and Fear Not

3. Then, again, I need not tell you that it is not always those who are most ready to go to war who are really the most patriotic. Sometimes, indeed, when all one's friends and neighbours are in favour of war, it requires more true bravery and true patriotism to speak up for peace than would be required even to go and fight in the war.

4. In the time of George III., more than a hundred years ago, the King and the Parliament wished to govern the English who had gone to America, and to govern them in a way which was contrary to their wishes and without their advice.

5. When the colonists—for so the English in America were then called—refused to obey a Parliament which they had not chosen, the King and the Parliament declared war upon them and sent soldiers to put them down. But there were some men in England who could not believe that it was right or just to make Englishmen obey laws which they themselves had had no share in making, and, despite the King and the majority of Parliament being against them, they had the courage to say so openly, and to try and obtain for their countrymen across the Atlantic the same rights which they claimed for themselves.

6. The greatest of these men was Edmund Burke, whose famous writings I hope you will read some day. Although many of his friends were anxious for war, and though by refusing to support the King he lost favour at court, he nevertheless raised his voice over and over again in favour of peace.

7. Unfortunately, he was not listened to; unluckily, those who cried out for war were listened to. The war went on; the colonists rose against the Royal troops and defeated them, and at last, as you know, the colonists refused any longer to submit to English rule and made a government and a nation of their own. That nation became the "United States of America."

8. It is impossible to say what would have been the future of England and the United States if the wise counsel of Edmund Burke

had been followed. But of one thing we may be sure: namely, that all the suffering and sorrow caused by an unjust war would have been avoided, and that the hatred and distrust which for a long time after the war existed between the English in England and the English in America would not have been felt.

9. Happily, the bitter memories of that time are long forgotten, and between England and the United States there are only feelings of friendship and brotherhood. But we can all see now how much better it would have been if Burke's words in favor of peace had prevailed; and we can see in him a true patriot because he was brave enough to say before all the world that he would not support what he thought to be unjust and wrong.

10. Thus you will see that there are many ways in which patriotism can be shown, and you will understand how necessary it is to distinguish true patriotism from that which is false.

11. Now that I have explained to you what is meant by being a good citizen, I shall give you some account of the different duties which a good citizen has to perform, of the laws by which he is governed, and of the advantages which he enjoys. I shall tell you how the laws are made and who it is that makes them. I shall show you how the country is defended from its enemies abroad and how good order and contentment are secured at home.

12. I want you also to learn something about the arrangements which are made for carrying out the law, for trying and punishing those who break it, and for protecting those who obey it.

CHAPTER III

HOW THE COUNTRY IS GOVERNED

"Now call we our high court of Parliament,
And let us choose such limbs of noble counsel,
That the great body of our state may go
In equal rank with the best govern'd nation."

Henry IV., Pt. ii., Act V., Sc. 2.

VII.
Who Governs

1. I TOLD you that before any one of us could be very useful citizens, it was necessary that we should know something of the laws of the country in which we live, should understand some of the chief reasons for those laws, and be acquainted with the ways in which they are made and carried out.

2. Many of you, as you will see when you read the next three chapters, will someday have to do with governing the country yourselves, and all of you will have to obey the laws by which it is governed. So it is really necessary that every boy and girl should learn as soon as possible something about these important matters.

3. How is the country governed? By the Government, is the first answer that you will be likely to give, and in a way, the answer is right. But who governs the Government? The answer is that Parliament does. But last of all, who governs Parliament? And the answer to that is that the people of this country govern Parliament. And so,

you will see that the real answer to the question, "Who governs the country?" is that "The country governs itself."

4. This was not always so. At one time the King alone governed the country; at another time, it was the King together with a few powerful lords. Until quite recently, although Parliament was supposed to decide all matters of government, Parliament itself was only elected by a few people, and so the country did not really govern itself. It is only quite lately that the vote has been given to almost every man of full age.

Parliament

5. But it is no use to go on talking about Governments and Parliaments and votes until we understand what Parliament really is and what a voter has got to do. I told you that the country really governed itself, but of course, it would be quite absurd to think that every man, whatever his position, and whatever his work, could really find time or be able to give orders and to arrange matters for the public good.

6. There is only one way in which all the millions of busy men who have their own living to get, and who yet wish to take some part in governing the country, can make their wishes known. Instead of going themselves to Parliament, they choose a man in whom they can trust to go there for them and to look after their interests when he gets there.

7. As you know, the man who is sent is called the *Member*, and those who send him are called his *Constituents* or *Electors*. Members who are elected in this way go to the *House of Commons*, which is one of the Houses of Parliament. There is another House of Parliament called the *House of Lords*, and above them both is the *Queen*. I shall tell you further on what is the work which has to be done by the Queen, the House of Lords, and the House of Commons in governing the country.

THE VICTORIA TOWER, HOUSE OF PARLIAMENT

The House of Commons

8. But first, we will try and learn a little more about the members of the House of Commons, and about the way in which they are elected; for, after all, it is the members of the House of Commons who speak not for themselves, but for the millions of people who elect them, who are the most important.

VIII.
Voting

1. Every man, when he grows up to be twenty-one and occupies a house, or lives in lodgings for which he pays £10 a year, has a vote; and there are many others who have no home of their own, nor yet pay £10 for their lodgings, who have the vote too. So, really, almost every boy may look forward to becoming an elector one day and giving his vote for a member of Parliament.

VOTING BY BALLOT FOR A NUMBER OF PARLIAMENT

2. Before the election time arrives, those who hope to be members of Parliament come down to the place for which they wish to be elected and tell the electors what their views are and what they intend to do when they get into Parliament. Then, when the day for giving the votes comes, the polling or voting begins. Each voter goes into the voting office and, without anyone seeing him, marks on a piece of paper a cross, X, opposite the name of the person whom he wishes to send to Parliament. This paper is called the "ballot" paper, and when he has marked it, he puts it into a big box with a hole in the top, which is called the "ballot-box."

BROWN, J..	
JONES, H. - X.	X
ROBINSON, C..	
SMITH, W..	

Here is a picture of the ballot paper:
You will see that the voter, in this case, has given his vote to Jones by marking his X opposite the name H. JONES on the paper.

3. At the end of the day, the ballot boxes are shut up and taken away to one place, where all the papers are opened and placed in separate heaps according to the names marked upon them. When they are all counted, the one who has the majority or largest number of votes is declared elected, and he becomes the member of Parliament for the place in which the election has been held.

4. Thus, if, on counting, the numbers are found to be -

Jones:..10,742   votes
Brown: 9,830   votes
Smith:...5,321   votes
Robinson: 942   votes

Then, if there is only one member to be elected, Jones will be the one chosen. Or, if there are two, then both Jones and Brown, the two highest, will become members. This is all that is done on the polling day—at least, it is all that you would see happen if you were at the polling station on the day of the election.

The Duty of Voters

5. But a great deal more has been done really, or at any rate, ought to have been done. For every single vote that has been given may make a difference to the country and may go to help or to harm it according to whether it is given in favour of a wise and honest member or in favour of one who goes to Parliament in a bad cause or without due care for the trust which has been given to him.

6. And here, I should like you to think for a moment how important it is that votes should be given carefully, and how seriously every voter ought to consider what he is doing when he folds up his paper and drops it into the ballot box. For by dropping his vote into the box, he is helping to elect a member of the British Parliament, and there is no body of men in the world who can do so much good or so much harm as the British Parliament.

7. When you remember that there is no corner of the world to which Englishmen have not found their way, and when you recollect that in the British Islands alone, there are nearly forty million people, and that every man, woman, and child among the millions across the sea and among the millions at home may be made happier or

unhappier according to whether the British Parliament is wise and far-seeing or foolish and hasty, you will understand how true this is.

8. And so, when you come to be voters, as most of you will, be sure to consider carefully what you do with your vote. Try and make sure that the man to whom you give it has some knowledge of the work he has got to do, for governing a great empire is no easy matter and requires special knowledge, just like making shoes or weaving cloth does.

9. Make sure, too, that he is going to Parliament with the intention of doing all he can for the country and not for himself or for his own friends. Sometimes men go into Parliament to make a name for themselves or to get advancement in life. But after all, they can only get into Parliament because the electors have chosen them, so it becomes the business of the electors to try and find out before they vote what their member really intends to do.

IX.
The Ballot.

1. You know I told you that when a voter went to the polling place, he marked his cross on the paper secretly, and no one could know by whom each separate paper was put into the box. This is done in order that each voter may vote according to his own true opinion and belief, and without fear or the hope of reward.

Bribery.

2. At one time, it was not uncommon for those who wished to become members of Parliament to pay money to the voters and to bribe them to vote in their favour. Sometimes also, they used to threaten to do some harm to the voters if they did not support them; for instance, they would threaten to turn them out of their houses, dismiss them from their employment, or injure their custom if they were shopkeepers, and by these and other means try to drive the

electors into voting, not because they wished to do so, but because they were afraid to refuse.

3. I am sorry to say that even now these things are done sometimes, but you will understand that under the ballot, when every man votes in secret, it is not very much use either to bribe or to threaten, for, after all, nobody knows when the voting is over who it is that has given each particular vote.

4. Thus, if a member of Parliament who was also the owner of a mill were to say nowadays to his workmen, "If you do not vote for me, I will punish you by turning you out of work," or if he were to go further and say, "If you will vote for me, I will give you a sum of money," he could never be certain after all whether those whom he threatened or those whom he bribed had really voted for or against him. So the ballot is really a great protection and helps people to vote exactly as they wish.

5. Of course, if everybody were quite honest, if members of Parliament were always ashamed to bribe or to threaten the voters, and the voters, on the other hand, were always too honest to receive bribes and too courageous to be afraid of threats, then there would be no need of the ballot, and everybody might vote openly and declare his opinions before all the world, which, indeed, would be much the best way. Only unfortunately, we cannot be sure that everybody will be both honest and courageous, so for the present, at any rate, we must keep to the plan of voting in secret.

6. The law says that it is very wrong to give or to receive bribes, and those who are discovered to have done either the one or the other are severely punished. This is not only law, but it is good sense, for to buy and sell votes is to buy and sell the happiness and prosperity of the country, to do an injury not only to ourselves but to all our countrymen, who are certain to suffer if people are sent to Parliament, not because they are wise and fit, but because they are rich and ready to use their riches in a bad way.

7. Now I have given you some account of how members of the House of Commons are elected. But you must not forget that besides the House of Commons, there is the House of Lords, and over both the House of Lords and the House of Commons, there is the Queen.

8. It is the Queen, Lords, and Commons who together make the laws by which we are all governed, and law-making is such an important thing that I had better begin a fresh chapter in order to tell you how these three together do the work which is entrusted to them.

CHAPTER IV.

QUEEN, LORDS, AND COMMONS.

"A land of settled government,
A land of just and old renown;
Where freedom slowly broadens down
From precedent to precedent."—*Tennyson*

X.

How Acts of Parliament Are Made

1. ALL government in our country is carried on according to law. Taxes are paid according to law; schools are built according to law; judges are appointed, and criminals are punished according to law. In short, in all we do, we are bound to act either according to law or, at any rate, not contrary to it.

2. How, then, is this law, which makes so much difference to all of us, fixed? It is fixed by Act of Parliament, and an Act of Parliament has to be passed by the Queen, the Lords, and the Commons.

The Queen.

3. The Queen is at the head of the Government of the country, and not of the British islands only, but of the whole British Empire. Queen Victoria is not like King Edward I or Queen Elizabeth, sovereign simply by the right of being the son or daughter of a king. She does not claim to rule over this Empire by right, but she is Queen because she is descended from King George III, who, in his turn, was

descended from George I, who was made King of Great Britain and Ireland by Parliament, that is to say, by the people of these islands.

4. Queen Victoria, therefore, reigns by the highest title that any king or queen can ever claim to reign by. She reigns by the will of

QUEEN VICTORIA
(Came to the Throne, June 20, 1837).
From a photograph by Messrs. Lafayette, of Dublin; taken in the 50th year of

the people. As long as the great majority of English people wish that she and her descendants should reign over them, so long will she and they be powerful and respected. Our Queen, unlike some of her ancestors, and unlike some other sovereigns, acts in all things in accordance with the laws of the land and in the interests of all her subjects alike.

5. The English people who live under her rule believe that they can be best governed by a king or queen. When we look at the steady and good government of this country, we see that the English people are right in their belief.

6. So long, therefore, as the Queen reigns by the will of her subjects, we are bound to honour and obey her. Queen Victoria we may love for her own sake, for she has always shown that she loved the nation over which she reigned; and besides loving her for her own sake, we should honour and obey her because she is accepted by many millions of our countrymen as the head of the Government.

The House of Lords.

7. I have told you what is the position of the Queen as sovereign of this country. Now let us turn to the two Houses of Parliament which join together with the Queen to make the laws by which we are governed. First, there is the House of Lords.

8. The House of Lords has a long history. It has been on the side of right, and it has been on the side of wrong in our past history. Most of the members of the House of Lords are men who have been rewarded for some service to the country by being made peers, or are the descendants of such men. For, strange though it may seem, the eldest son of a man who has thus been rewarded becomes a lord, too, after his father's death, and his son in turn succeeds him; and so it goes on till, in some cases, men sit in the House of Lords whose ancestors have sat there for two or three hundred years back.

9. Others there are whose ancestors were made lords for bad and shameful reasons, either because they were the favourites of the king or because they or their relatives had done some service to the king, services for which they deserved little thanks from the country. Whenever there have been bad kings, there have always been bad men

brought into the House of Lords, and they too, like those who have really done well and served the country faithfully, handed down to their children the power to help make laws for the whole people.

10. Besides the members who have been made lords for their services, good or bad, or who are born lords because of the services which their forefathers rendered, there are others who are appointed for their life only, and whose business it is to help the other lords in deciding hard points of law. These are called the Law Lords. Their sons do not succeed them when they die. In the House of Lords also sit two archbishops and twenty-four bishops.

11. At the head of the House of Lords is the Lord Chancellor, who sits on a great red seat in the middle of the House called the wool-sack. He it is who keeps order when questions are being discussed.

The House of Commons

12. Lastly comes the House of Commons, the members of which, as you already know, are elected by all the people of the United Kingdom. The "Speaker" of the House of Commons is like the Lord Chancellor in the House of Lords; he keeps order and settles any disputes which may arise.

13. Both the House of Lords and the House of Commons are arranged in such a way that the members sit facing each other on either side. The party that sits on one side is called the Government Party, and that which sits on the other is called the Opposition. In the picture, you will see how the House of Commons is arranged. The seats on the left of the picture are called the Government benches, and those on the right are the Opposition benches. In the big chair at the end sits the Speaker. Now that we have got some notion of what is meant by Queen, Lords, and Commons, we can go on and see what it is they each of them do, and how it is they make laws between them.

THE HOUSE OF COMMONS.

XI.
How Laws Are Made

1. Before a law can be made, someone either in the House of Commons or in the House of Lords must bring in what is called a *Bill*, that is to say, a printed statement of the new law he wishes to make, or of the alteration in the old law which he desires. Bills which, if they are passed, will compel people to pay taxes can only be brought forward in the House of Commons, and the House of Lords cannot alter them. For it is plainly fair that those who have to pay the money

should decide how it is to be got, and it is the electors who elect the House of Commons who really have to pay in the long run.

2. When a Bill has been brought in, it is debated and talked over by both parties, and it is altered first in one way and then in another. If the members cannot agree about any point, then the House divides, that is to say, all who think one way go out at one door, and those who think the other way go out at another. As they go out, they are counted, and the majority, that is to say, the greater number, get their way.

An Act of Parliament

MEMBERS OF THE HOUSE
OF COMMONS VOTING.

3. When all the alterations that anyone wants to make are settled, then the Bill itself is read and voted upon. Before it is allowed to pass altogether, a Bill has to be read and passed by a majority three times, both in the House of Lords and in the House of Commons. For a Bill that is brought in in the Lords has to pass through the Commons afterwards, and one that is brought in in the Commons has to go afterwards through the Lords.

The Royal Assent

4. When both Houses have passed the Bill, it goes before the Queen, and she has to assent to it or refuse it. Really, when a Bill has passed through both Houses of Parliament, the Queen always gives her assent, for you must remember that our present Queen, unlike some of her ancestors—unlike Elizabeth or Charles I, for instance—follows the advice of her Ministers in Parliament. So, what her Ministers have approved, the Queen approves too.

The Law of the Land

5. When the Queen has approved of the Bill, or, as the phrase goes, when the Royal Assent has been given to it, the Bill becomes an Act, and from that time forward, it is part of the law of the land, which you and I are bound to obey until it is altered. Now that you understand how carefully laws are made and how they have to be considered and approved by the chosen representatives of the people, you will see how wrong it is to try and evade or break the law, still more how wrong it is to try and alter it by force.

6. There was a time when the laws were made by a few only and were often made only for the benefit of a few. Then there may often have been an excuse for resisting by force rules and regulations which hardly anybody had been consulted about.

The Law Must Be Obeyed

7. In those days, if men rebelled against the law, they were called traitors to the king, and when they were caught, if the king was strong enough, he used to punish them. Now, however, that the laws are made by all for the benefit of all, anybody who tries by force to break them or set them aside is a traitor not to the Queen only but to his country and to his countrymen who have made the law which he is bad enough to break. Therefore, you see, in England, it must always be wrong to use force or violence or to disobey the law.

8. I do not mean that all the laws that are made are good ones or that we shall be wise in always resting content with the laws as they are. On the contrary, there are many laws which are bad in themselves, and there are many others which become useless or old-fashioned as times change.

9. But if a law be bad, or if it be no longer needed, there is one way, and one way only, in which it can rightly be altered or got rid of, that is by persuading the majority of voters that it is bad or out of date and getting them, through their members of Parliament, to change it or to do away with it. In a free country, a law must be obeyed until it is altered. It can only be altered by Act of Parliament. Every man who tries to alter it by any other means is a traitor to his country.

CHAPTER V.

HOW THE LAWS ARE CARRIED OUT.

"Every purpose is established by counsel."—*Proverbs* XX. 18

XII.
Public Offices

1. YOU have heard that the country is governed by Parliament, that is to say, that Parliament makes the laws by which we are all governed. But when laws are made, there is still something to be done before they can be of much use, and that is that they should be put into practice.

2. In order to see that the laws are put into practice, and that all the arrangements made by Parliament are carried out in the best way, a large number of persons are employed in what are called the *public offices*. At the head of each public office is a *Minister*, who is usually a member of Parliament. It is his business to see that everything goes right in his office, and that all things are done which may be necessary for properly carrying on the particular work with which he is charged. There are a large number of public offices. I will tell you something about the most important ones.

The Home Office

3. First, there is the *Home Office*, at the head of which is the *Home Secretary*. It is the business of the Home Secretary to look after the magistrates, to appoint inspectors for coal mines and

factories, and to arrange a great many other things which have to do with carrying out the law in Great Britain and Ireland. One of the most important and difficult things which the Home Secretary has to do is to advise the Queen when she ought to pardon those who have been condemned to death by the law or to make their sentence less severe.

4. It sometimes happens that after a man has been tried and found guilty, some new thing may be discovered which proves him to be less guilty than was supposed, or may show him to be altogether innocent. In such a case, the Home Secretary may advise the Queen to lessen the punishment or to pardon the prisoner altogether.

5. Of course, it is a very serious thing for any man, whether he be a Home Secretary or anyone else, to make up his mind what is right in such cases, for where a judge and a jury have been agreed about a crime, it must always be very difficult for any one man to

THE ADMIRALTY

TOWN HALL, MELBOURNE

set aside their decision. For this reason, no Home Secretary will ever interfere with the sentence of the law without a very strong and clear reason.

The Admiralty and War Office

6. Two very important offices are the *Admiralty* and the *War Office*, which, as you will suppose, are entrusted with the care of the navy and the army. The Minister at the head of the former is called the *First Lord of the Admiralty*; the head of the War Office is the *Secretary of State for War*.

The Colonial Office

7. A very important office indeed is the *Colonial Office*. The Minister at the head of it is called the *Colonial Secretary*, and it is his business to see to everything that concerns the colonies. When you look at the map and see what great countries Canada, Australia, and New Zealand are, and when you remember that the people who

CAPE TOWN

live in them are countrymen of our own, with all our English love of liberty and fair play, you will understand how important it is that the Colonial Secretary should be both friendly and wise in all that he has to do with the people of these great countries.

SOME OF THE QUEEN'S BLACK SUBJECTS (HINDU LABOURERS).

8. And there is another very important thing which the Colonial Secretary has to do sometimes. You will see on the map that besides the great colonies of Canada and Australia, there are others, such as the Cape Colony and Jamaica, which are very important too, but which, as your geography books will tell you, contain a great number of people who are not English at all. At the Cape, there are a great many descendants of the Dutch people, to whom Cape Town once belonged, and besides the Dutch, there are many hundreds of thousands of natives—Caffres, Zulus, Swazis, and other black races—who are now under the government of the Queen.

9. In the same way, in Jamaica, besides the English inhabitants, there are many thousands of negroes, the descendants of the old slaves. Now, it has been found that wherever Englishmen and black men live together in the same country, there is a great danger of the English or white men acting cruelly or unfairly to

the natives or blacks unless great care is taken to prevent their so acting. But it would be very wrong if, under the rule of England, people were made to suffer merely because their skins were black, or were treated unfairly by the law because they were weak and could not protect themselves.

10. As I told you, everyone, whether he be black or white, is equal before the law. But it is often necessary for the Colonial Secretary to watch very closely and carefully what is being done by Englishmen to the natives and black people in our colonies. It is his business to try and give equal justice to all, and we at home ought to try and support him in doing what is sometimes very difficult.

The Foreign Office

11. The *Foreign Office* has to look after all business with foreign countries. At its head is the *Secretary of State for Foreign Affairs*, or Foreign Secretary, as he is sometimes called. It is his business to make arrangements between this country and all foreign nations and to see that Englishmen abroad are fairly and justly treated according to the laws of the country in which they happen to be. His work is very important, for sometimes it is he who really decides what answer shall be sent to the foreign minister of another country when there is any matter in dispute, and sometimes it happens that peace or war depends upon his answer.

Ambassadors.

12. In all the great countries of the world, there are persons specially appointed to look after the affairs of the British Empire, and to explain to the governments of other countries the wishes and intentions of our own Government and our own Parliament. These persons are called *Ambassadors or Ministers*, and it is to them that the Foreign Secretary sends the messages which he wishes to be

delivered. The Ambassador of England is supposed to stand in the place of the Queen in the country to which he is sent. He is treated with great respect because it is known that when he speaks, he speaks in the name of a great country.

13. In the same way, other countries—Germany, France, Austria, and so on—have their ambassadors in London, who, like our own ambassadors abroad, are treated with great respect and are held in high honour. When two nations go to war, they call their ambassadors home, and this is a sign that they are no longer on friendly terms with each other.

XIII.
Other Offices

1. Besides the offices I have mentioned, there are many others. There is the *Local Government Board*, which looks after the relief of the poor and the keeping up of workhouses and does all things necessary to carry out the laws which are intended to secure healthy arrangements. If cholera threatens to break out in this country, it is the duty of this office to prevent the infection from being spread and to provide hospitals for those who are sick.

2. Then there is the *Education Office*, which sees that the law is carried out which says that all children shall be sent to school, and that the money given by Parliament for schools is properly spent.

The Post Office

3. And there are also the *Post Office* and the *Telegraph Office*, which between them manage the whole of the wonderful arrangements by which letters and telegrams can be sent safely not only from one end of England to the other, but round the world—to China, to India, to America, to Australia, and to every corner of the globe.

4. It is hard to understand how enormous is the quantity of

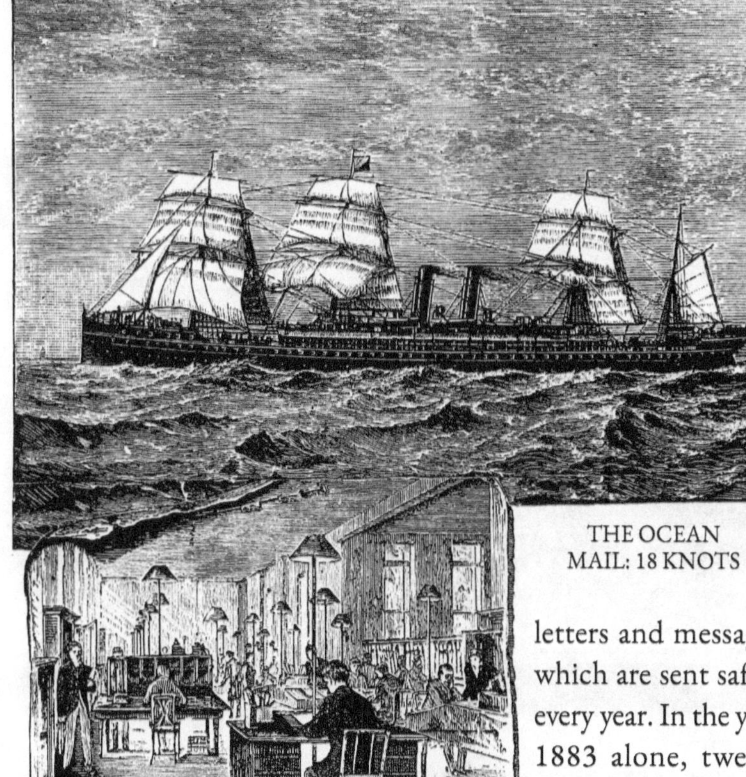

THE OCEAN
MAIL: 18 KNOTS

INSIDE A GOVERNMENT OFFICE.

letters and messages which are sent safely every year. In the year 1883 alone, twelve hundred and eighty-two million letters were delivered in the United Kingdom. And not only letters and newspapers, but no less than thirty-two million pounds of money was forwarded in one way or another through the Post Office. In another chapter, I shall tell you something of the savings banks which are managed by the Post Office and which are a great help to all those who are wise enough to wish to save money for a rainy day. But now I will only tell you one or two things which will interest you about the posting and stamping of letters.

THE MAIL TRAIN: SIXTY MILES AN HOUR

The Penny Post

5. As you know, any of you now can send a letter from "John O'Groat's House" to the Land's End for a penny, and a postcard or a newspaper for a halfpenny. Fifty years ago, things were very different; every letter cost from sixpence to a shilling, and very many people were unable to afford to write letters at all.

6. It was not till 1840 that Sir Rowland Hill first saw that not only could letters be carried for a penny without loss, but that by making it so easy for everyone to write and receive letters, the number of stamps used and letters sent would be enormously increased. By persuading Parliament to try his plan, he conferred a very great boon

upon the people of the United Kingdom—a boon which you and I get the benefit of every time we put a penny stamp upon a letter and send it through the post.

The Blind Postmaster

7. I am tempted to tell you something about one other Englishman who did great service to us all by his work at the Post Office. You will see on this a picture of Mr. Fawcett, the blind Postmaster-General, who died in 1884. I mention him in the first place because by the many improvements he made in the working of the Post Office, he has earned the right to be remembered as a good and useful minister. And in the second place, I mention him because both by his life and by his work, he gave an example to all his countrymen of what may be done, even under the greatest difficulties and the most terrible affliction, by one who is devoted to the service of his country.

Public Examinations

8. There are other offices, for instance, the *Exchequer*, which looks after the collection of taxes and the payment of money to the Army, the Navy, and to everyone to whom the country has to pay money. All those who are employed in the Government offices are called Civil Servants,

THE BLIND POSTMASTER

and to enter the Civil Service, everyone has to pass an examination to show that he is fitted for the work that he or she has got to do.

9. This used not to be always so. At one time, places were given not to the cleverest or most deserving, but to those who had powerful friends to help them. It is a very good thing that the change has been made, for it is most important that the work of the country should be done in the best possible way by those who are most fitted by their knowledge and industry to do it.

CHAPTER VI

OUR LITTLE PARLIAMENTS.

"The greatest trust between man and man is the
trust of giving counsel."—*Bacon.*

XIV.
County Councils

1. You have heard about Parliament, how it is elected, and how
it makes laws for the whole country. You have seen also how the
Ministers and those who are put under them in the different offices
carry out the laws which are made by Parliament.

2. But besides the laws which are required for the whole country,
and which are the same for all parts of it, there are other regulations
which have to be made for the government of different counties and
towns, which are not the same in all places. The wants of one county
or one town may differ from those of another, and those who live
on the spot will know best what the wants of each place are.

3. Parliament has, therefore, passed a law giving to the inhabitants of each county or large town in England the right to elect a
little Parliament or Council of their own to do the work required
for the proper government of their particular district. None of
these little Parliaments can make any law or rule which is contrary
to a law made by the Parliament of the United Kingdom, and they
can only concern themselves with such matters as are entrusted to
them by Parliament.

How They Are Elected

4. The Councils of which I have been speaking are a new thing in this country. It was only in the year 1888 that an Act of Parliament was passed, by which these Councils were set up in every county and in all the most important towns of Great Britain. They are called *County Councils* and are composed of members elected in the same way as members of Parliament are elected. But while lodgers may

LORD ROSEBERY
The first *Chairman* of the
London County Council.

vote for members of Parliament and women may not, in the County Councils it is just the other way: the lodgers may not vote, and the women may vote.

5. The number of members on a County Council varies according to the size and importance of the county or town which is represented by the Council. The little county of Rutland has twenty-one members; the big county of Yorkshire has two hundred and ten. Some large counties are divided into districts, each of which has a County Council of its own, and all the counties and districts are divided into smaller divisions, each of which elects one member.

6. Besides the members, or "Councillors," who are elected, there are in each Council a certain number of "Aldermen," one alderman for every two councillors. The aldermen are not elected but are chosen by the councillors. They may either be taken from the number of those who have been elected, in which case fresh councillors have to be elected to fill the places of those who are chosen as aldermen; or they may be taken from outside the Council altogether. The council-

lors are elected for three years, and the aldermen for six years, but half of the aldermen have to give up their office at the end of three years.

7. It is a wise plan to allow some of the members to keep their places for six years, for if the whole number were changed every three years, the Council would take up nearly the whole of its time in learning how to do its work.

What They Do

8. The County Councils have a great deal of work to do.

They have to look after the highroads and the police[3]. They take care of the lunatic asylums and reformatory schools. They collect the rates paid by the people living in the district, and they have many other important duties to perform.

XV.
The True Work of the County Council

1. The work of the County Councils is in one way very different from the work of Parliament, for though part of their business is to make laws and regulations, by far the most important thing they have to do is to carry out the laws which are already made. For this reason, it is most important that only those persons should be elected to the County Councils who have experience in business and who are hard workers. A man who only makes speeches and gives no attention to business is even more useless in a County Council than in Parliament itself.

Old Friends with New Faces

2. I have said that County Councils are quite new, and in their present shape, they certainly are so. But it is interesting to notice how in this matter, as in many others, English people prefer to go

3   Except in London, where the police are not under the County Council. In the City of London, they are under the Lord Mayor and Corporation. Outside the City, they are under the Home Secretary.

back to some old custom or to some old institution in their past history, and to make it the model for their action rather than to create something quite new and strange.

3. The very plan of having County Councils elected by the people in the county to do the work of the county is at least a thousand years old. And not only the plan itself but the very names of the districts to which the Councils belong and of the persons who are elected to take part in them are to be found in the history of England long before the time of William the Conqueror. If we take up a newspaper today, we may see that Mr. So-and-so has been chosen as an alderman for the district of Lindsey, or that the County Councils for the Soke of Peterborough and the Isle of Ely have met to do business.

4. But if we turn from the newspaper to the Anglo-Saxon Chronicle—a history of England, a great part of which was written in the time of King Alfred the Great, who, as you know, was born in the year 849—we find the very names and the very places which we have just seen in the newspaper of today. We find how the *Aldermen* or *Eldermen* were the leaders of the people in peace and war; we find accounts of the Lindiswarras, or people of Lindsey, the same Lindsey which now gives its name to the County Council district; we find the Isle of Ely; and the very name of the Soke of Peterborough takes us back to Saxon times, for soke is itself a Saxon word and comes from soc, which means the right of holding a court or council[4]. And, indeed, there were County Councils too—or, as they were then called, "Folk Moots," or People's Councils—the members of which were elected to do the business of the county just as the new County Councillors of the present day are elected for the same purpose.

4   The word soon came to mean the district over which the court or council exercised its rights.

A Good Old Way, the English Plan

5. And these are not the only examples. All over England, we shall find names which were as familiar to our forefathers a thousand years ago as they are to us at the present day. And so it is true that in making our County Councils, we have once more followed the good old English plan of keeping all that was worthy and useful in the work of the past, and adding to it and shaping it so as to be useful for our present needs.

CHAPTER VII

LAW AND JUSTICE.

"In the first class I place the judges as of the first importance. It is
the public justice that holds the community together."

—Burke.

XVI.
The Old Plan and the New

1. IN all civilized countries in the world, there are courts of justice
and judges whose duty it is to decide disputes between people who
are unable to agree about their rights, and to try and to punish those
who break the law.

2. In savage and uncivilized countries only are there no judges
to be found; in such places, disputes are still settled by force, those
who are strongest taking what they desire from others who are too
weak to resist. In the early history of England, you will find a time
when the same bad plan was followed, and when, instead of bringing
their claim before a magistrate or a judge, men chose rather to adopt:

> "The good old way, the ancient plan—
> To let him take who hath the power,
> And let him keep who can."

3. You will not require to think very long before you see that
this "good old way" was, in reality, a very bad way. In fact, so long
as people try to settle their own quarrels and their own disputes in

the way they themselves think right, there will never be peace and contentment in a country.

The "Bad" Old Way

4. And so it is too with the punishment of those who commit crimes. There was a time in England when, if one man killed another, the friends and relations of the murdered man used to arm themselves and attack the home of the murderer and try to take his life. Of course, it sometimes happened that the friends of the criminal were more powerful than those of the injured man, and that the party which had right on their side were beaten, and matters became even worse than they were before.

5. And, indeed, whichever side was successful, the result was bad for those who themselves undertook to revenge injuries which they or their friends had suffered, and forgot the two great rules which at all times we should bear in mind -

Two Rules

First—"That no one should be a judge in his own cause."

And, secondly—"That no one should take the law into his own hands."

6. In order that these two important rules should be observed, the plan has been adopted in all civilized countries of appointing certain persons to hear and decide upon all disputes, and to try all offenders. These persons, as you know, are judges and magistrates, to whom is given power to give decisions and to award punishments.

The Judges

7. It is necessary that the judges should do their work without fear or favor, and with perfect fairness. For this reason, they are appointed for their whole life and can only be dismissed for bad conduct, when a request is made to the Queen by Parliament to do so.

8. By being thus appointed for life, the judges are more likely to be perfectly fair, for they can look forward to no further favor and can give all their thought and all their strength to doing their own work well, without having to think of how they may best provide for themselves as they would have to in case they were made to give way to other men after they had served for a few years only.

The Work of the Judge

9. It is not the business of the judges to make the law; that, you remember, is done by Parliament. But what they have to do is to decide whether the laws that Parliament has made have been broken, and whether the rules Parliament has approved of have been obeyed.

10. Besides this, they have to say what punishment shall be given to those who break the law. But you must not suppose that the judge or the magistrate can give what punishment he likes; on the contrary, he is only allowed to punish each crime according to the rules laid down by law. For instance:—Supposing two men were to break into a house and rob the people to whom the house belonged.

11. When it is proved that they are guilty of the crime, the law says they may both be punished by being sent to prison for 14 years. It may turn out, however, that one of the two men has often been sent to prison before, and that the other has always had a good character but has been led away by his comrade. Then the judge would send the one to prison for the whole 14 years, as long as the law would allow, but the other he would probably send to prison for six months only, in the hope that he might profit by the lesson and lead an honest life afterward. So you will see that the judge has the right to vary the punishment, but he can never punish any man beyond what the law permits.

The Jury

12. I have been talking to you all this time about the judges only; but, as I dare say most of you know, in a court of justice, besides the judge, there is generally the jury. What is the jury? What is the use of it? And what does it do?

13. When a prisoner is to be tried, twelve men are chosen by lot out of a long list of people living in the neighborhood, and it is their business to hear all that is said for and against the prisoner, to listen to what the judge tells them about the law, and then to say whether they think the prisoner be "guilty or not guilty." These men are called jurymen; and every Englishman has the right to be tried by a jury.

The Use of the Jury

14. The great use of a jury is to make sure that no prisoner shall be punished unjustly, or let off unjustly, only because the persons who hear his case are his enemies or his friends. You will see that if the judge only were to decide, it is possible that he might be led to do so unfairly because he disliked the prisoner, or because he was a friend of the man whom the prisoner had injured, or for some other personal reason. But when twelve men are taken by chance out of a great number, it is very unlikely—indeed, it is almost impossible—that they should all be friends or enemies of the prisoner. It is much more likely that they will be fair to both sides. And in this way, juries help the cause of right and justice.

15. When a man is tried by a jury in England or Ireland, it is the rule that all the jurymen must be agreed before he is pronounced "guilty" or "not guilty." In Scotland, the jury numbers fifteen, and the rule is that the majority decide—that is, if eight out of the fifteen think that the prisoner has committed the crime with which he is charged, then he is declared guilty.

16. The decision of the jury is called their "verdict"; and when

the verdict has been given, then it is the turn of the judge to pronounce the sentence and to give the punishment. In the next chapter, I shall give you an account of a trial before a judge and jury, and shall try and explain to you the rules by which the work of justice is done.

THE TRIAL

"The law is no respecter of persons."

XVII.
Maxims

1. I AM now going to give you an account of a trial in a Court of Justice before a judge. But first, you must learn some of the great rules which are observed in Courts of Justice wherever the law of England is carried out. They are four in number, and are as follows -

i. Everyone is equal before the law.

ii. Every man is held to be innocent until he is proved to be guilty.

iii. No man can be tried twice for the same offense.

iv. All Courts of Justice are open to the public.

To these four great rules, you should add the other two which you have already learned. They are –

v. No one is a judge in his own cause.

vi. No one has the right to take the law into his own hands.

2. Now we have got our rules, let us see how they work.

The Crime

Let us suppose that a robbery has been committed, and that some silver spoons have been stolen from a house during the daytime.

3. The police find out first all they can about the theft. They ask questions from the owner of the house; they examine all the people

who were about at the time of the robbery. At last, they learn enough to make them suspect a particular man, and they go to the magistrate for a warrant or order to allow them to take him prisoner, for unless they see a man actually committing a crime, not even the police can take him prisoner without such a warrant.

4. The next thing that happens is that the prisoner is himself brought before the magistrates, and if it appears to the magistrates that the police have fair reason to think that the prisoner is the real thief, then they will commit him for trial—that is to say, they will send him back to prison to wait until the judge comes to try him. Where only small crimes have been committed, the magistrates may themselves try the prisoner, and if they find that he is guilty, they may send him to prison; but all the more serious crimes are tried by the judges.

5. When the prisoner is sent back to prison to wait for his trial, he is only shut up and kept safe; he is not made to do hard work like those who have been tried and found guilty, for, as I told you in Rule 2, *"Every man is held to be innocent until he is proved to be guilty."*

The Accusation

6. After a time, the Assizes[5] begin: that is to say, the judges come to the town and begin to try the prisoners. But first of all, the case of each prisoner is brought before what is called the Grand Jury, which is a body of twenty-three men whose business it is to say whether or not there is any real proof that the accused persons are guilty of the crimes with which they are charged. If the Grand Jury thinks that the case has been trumped up, or that no one can really say whether the accused persons did what they are charged with or not, then they have the right to stop the case going to the judge at all, and the prisoner is set free.

5   "Assizes" mean sittings.

The Court

7. But if, as usually happens, they think that at any rate there is some reason for believing that the police are right, and that they have got hold of the real criminal, then they send in the case to be tried by the judge and jury in court. At last, the name of the prisoner who is accused of robbing the house is called out, and he is brought into court. In front of him sits the judge in his wig and robes, and on one side of the judge sit the jury, twelve in number, chosen by lot out of

JUDGE AND JURY.

a large number of persons living in the neighborhood. The prisoner himself is put into the "dock" where he is guarded by policemen.

8. But this is not all; for besides the judge, the jury, and the prisoner, you will see two or three men in wigs and black gowns sitting opposite the judge. These are the lawyers, whose business it is to show what the case is against the prisoner, and to prove, if they can, that he is guilty, on the one hand, and those whose business it is to defend the prisoner, and to try and prove him innocent, on the other. The first are called counsel for the Crown, which means the Government, or counsel for the prosecution; the second are the counsel for the prisoner.

XVIII.
The Lawyers.

1. You will, perhaps, think it strange that it should be necessary to have lawyers at all, and that it would be better to let the prisoner speak for himself, and to let the people who saw him commit the crime speak against him. But this would not really be the best way. It has been found that justice is best done when this plan of having men who know the law to ask questions on both sides is adopted. In this way, everything that can be said against the prisoner, and everything that can be said in his favor, is said, and when both sides have done all they can, then the jury and the judge are able to make up their minds as to where the real truth lies.

2. Sometimes, indeed, a prisoner likes to speak for himself without the help of any lawyer, and he always has the right to do so. But in the greater number of cases, he does not use this right; and he is wise in not doing so, for few people, whether they be innocent or guilty, are able to keep their thoughts quite clear when they are brought up in court and accused of a crime. Moreover, it is difficult even for clever and educated people to ask and answer all the questions which

THE PRISONER AND HIS COUNSEL.

may be necessary; and they are much more likely to do themselves harm than good by trying.

3. The rest of the court is filled up with people who wish to hear the trial, and if there be room, you or I may go in and stop there as long as we behave ourselves respectfully and quietly, for "*All courts of justice are open to the public.*"

The Judge.

4. But before I begin to tell you about the trial, I want you to notice one or two things about the court. First of all, when the judge comes in, everybody rises from his seat as a mark of respect, and everyone, no matter who he may be, takes off his hat, and keeps it off, as long as the judge is present. This is right, for the judge, who is doing his work for the good of all the people, deserves our respect; and there is no one in the land who ought not to feel, and to show that he feels, this respect, for *"Everyone is equal before the law."*

The Story of Judge Gascoigne and Prince Henry.

5. Those of you who remember your English history will know the story of Judge Gascoigne and Prince Henry. It is a good lesson to us of the duty of the judge to make the law respected, and of the duty of every man, rich and poor alike, to submit to the law. Prince Henry, who afterwards became Henry V of England, was in his youth a wild scapegrace, accustomed to live with bad companions, and often mixed up in unworthy brawls.

6. One day it happened that one of the Prince's companions was brought up before Chief-Justice Gascoigne for the commission of some crime. The young Prince, angry at his friend's capture, and believing that, as a son of the king and heir to the throne, he would be able to terrify the Chief Justice, appeared in court, and with threatening words laid his hand upon his sword, and ordered the judge to release the prisoner.

7. But Gascoigne was mindful of the duties of his office, and remembered that the law is no respecter of persons. So far from releasing the prisoner, he gave orders that Henry himself should be committed to gaol for daring to insult one of the judges of the land. To prison, therefore, the Prince went, according to the story; and, to his credit, it is said that, so far from blaming the act of the

PRINCE HENRY BEFORE JUDGE GASCOIGNE.

judge, he recognized and honored the courage and wisdom which Gascoigne had shown.

8. When his father, King Henry IV, was told of what had happened, he said, "Happy is the king who possesses a judge so resolute in the discharge of his duty, and a son so willing to yield to the authority of the law." So true is it that justice which is not equal for all alike is no justice at all.

9. But let us get back to the trial, and see what takes place.

The Jury.

First of all, the jury are made to take an oath to "well and truly try" the question which is to come before them. Those who think that it is wrong to take an oath are allowed to make a solemn promise, which, of course, is really quite as binding as the oath, and which it would be quite as wrong to break.

The Trial.

10. Then the trial begins. First, the counsel for the prosecution tells the jury the history of the crime, why it is that the prisoner is suspected of having committed it, and how he is going to prove that he did. For everything must be proved, because, as you remember, every man *is held to be innocent until he is proved to be guilty*. So that however sure the judge and jury might be that the prisoner was really guilty, the law would not allow them to condemn him unless what they thought was proved to be true.

The Witnesses.

11. When the counsel has finished his speech, he begins to call his witnesses; that is to say, he calls and questions all the people who have seen the crime committed, or who have seen things which happened before or after it, and which make it likely that the prisoner was the real criminal. For instance, one witness may say that he saw the door

of the house open just before the spoons were stolen. Another may say that he saw the prisoner running down the street just after. And a third may say that on another day, the prisoner offered to sell him some silver spoons. Now, none of these things alone would show much, but taken altogether, they show a good deal.

12. You must notice, however, that no witness is allowed to speak about, or as it is called, to give evidence about that which he has only heard from others. It is what he has himself seen, and what he knows himself that he is allowed to tell when he is giving evidence which may end in sending another man to prison.

13. It is well to remember this rule, and indeed we shall do well to make it a rule for ourselves, and to be very careful how we believe mere hearsay or report, whatever it may be about, and especially if it be anything to the discredit of others. The greatest injustice has often been done by believing evil too readily, and the law is very wise in laying it down as a rule that *"hearsay evidence shall not be received."*

14. Each witness, as he comes forward, is made, like the juryman, to take an oath, or else to solemnly affirm that he will *"Tell the truth, the whole truth, and nothing but the truth,"* and if he intentionally tells more than the truth, or less than the truth, or what is untrue, he commits a crime against law called perjury, and which we sometimes speak of as bearing false witness, and for that crime, he may be severely punished, for it is necessary that, above all things, truth, and truth only, should be spoken in a Court of Justice.

XIX.
The Prisoner's Case.

1. As soon as the counsel for the prosecution has finished questioning each witness, the counsel for the prisoner again questions him in order to show, if he can, that what he has said is incorrect, or that he has said less or more than the witness really knows, or that he has left out something which is in the prisoner's favor. Then the

NEWGATE GAOL.

first counsel asks a few more questions so as to allow the witness to correct any mistakes he may have made, and then the next witness is called; this goes on till all the witnesses for the prosecution have been examined.

2. Then comes the turn of the prisoner's counsel; he calls witnesses favorable to his side. He may, for instance, call someone who proves that the prisoner was in another part of the town when the robbery was committed, or that the spoons he sold were the prisoner's own property, or anything else which helps to show that the prisoner is innocent. All these witnesses are cross-examined in their turn, just as the others were, only this time by the counsel for the prosecution, and like them, are re-examined.

3. Then the prisoner's counsel makes a speech, in which he goes through all that has been said, for and against the prisoner, and tries

to show that what has been said in his favor is to be believed, and that what has been said against him is untrue. Last of all comes the speech of the counsel for the prosecution, who does the same thing, but puts matters in another light, so as to show the jury that after all, the prisoner is guilty.

The "Summing Up" and Verdict.

4. If matters stopped here, you may fancy that the poor jury would find it a very hard task to make up their minds after so much had been said on both sides, but luckily there is the judge to help them; it is now time for him to "sum up," that is to say, to go through all that has been said on *both* sides, to guide the jury, to show them what evidence is important, and what is unimportant, and to explain to them what the law says about the crime.

5. Then the jury consult together, and when they are agreed (see p. 59), their leader, or foreman, is asked by the Clerk of the Court to say whether the jury find the prisoner "Guilty, or not guilty." If the verdict be "Guilty," the judge will then sentence the prisoner to be sent to gaol, and to be kept to hard labour. If, on the other hand, the verdict be "Not guilty," then the prisoner will walk out of the court a free man, and whatever may happen, he will never be in danger of being charged again with the robbery, for "*No man can be tried twice for the same offence.*"

6. Such is the way in which a trial is conducted in a court of justice. From beginning to end, everything is done for the purpose of finding out the truth, the whole truth, and nothing but the truth, of letting the innocent go free, and of punishing the guilty.

Criminal and Civil Trials.

7. I have now given you the account of the trial of a prisoner; you must not think, however, that all the time of the judges, the lawyers, and the juries is taken up with trying prisoners for crimes

they have committed. There is another kind of work which they have to do, which is nearly as important, and which takes up a great deal of their time.

8. When I told you that in old days, and in savage countries, men settled their disputes by force, and without justice or a fair trial, I spoke not only of revenging crimes, such as murder or theft, but of settling disputes as to people's rights, and deciding questions where two men claimed the same thing, and as we now use our judges and juries to punish criminals, so we also use them to settle disputes between those who cannot agree.

A Criminal Trial.

9. Thus, if, as in the previous chapter, a man is accused of stealing, he is brought before a judge and tried for his crime, and that is called a *Criminal Trial*, and the court in which the trial takes place is called a *Criminal Court*.

A Civil Trial.

10. But if, for instance, two men are unable to decide to whom a particular field or house belongs, or suppose that one man has bought a horse from another, and the buyer will not pay the money although he has got the horse, then in each case they will bring the matter before a judge, and he will try it, and will decide which is in the right, to whom the field belongs, or whether the man who bought the horse ought to pay the money. Such a trial as this is called a *Civil Trial*, and the court in which it is held is called a *Civil Court*.

11. I hope you will now see the difference between *criminal* and *civil* law. The first has to do with the punishment of all those who commit crimes against the law, such as murder, robbery, perjury, theft, and many other offences. The second has to do with the settlement of disputes about the rights of people who cannot agree, and these disputes may arise in hundreds of ways, about rent, about buying and

selling, about doing harm to other people's property, about wills, by which people leave their money after their death—in short, about every question of a man's rights which he cannot decide for himself.

12. All these may give rise to what are called civil actions—that is to say, trials for the purpose of finding out the rights of either side.

CHAPTER VIII.—PART II.

THE AUTHORITY OF THE LAW.

"The majesty and power of law and justice."—
Henry IV., Part 2, Act 5, Scene 2.

XX.
The Power of the Judges.

1. I HAVE told you, and indeed you all know, that those who are proved before a court of justice to have broken the law are punished by being sent to prison. Those who have wilfully and unlawfully taken the life of another man are themselves put to death by the law.

2. It is a very terrible thing to be deprived of liberty even for a day; it is far more terrible to be shut up in prison for months, for years, and in some cases for a whole lifetime. For one man to take the life of another, even for the best reason in the world, is a very solemn thing. If anybody were to do any of these things out of revenge, they would be altogether bad, and nothing could excuse the man who took such a course.

Punishments.

3. In the first place, revenge is altogether wrong and forbidden by our religion. In the second place, punishments that were intended only to hurt the person who had done wrong would be of very little good. The only way in which punishments can be made really useful is by taking care that they shall be an example and a warning to others, so that they may not commit the crime which the law

74

has condemned. To put it quite shortly, *all punishments should be preventive.*

4. In this way, the imprisonment to which a thief or a false witness is sentenced is useful in helping other people, and in warning them against crimes which lead to such a punishment.

5. And so we come round again to the explanation which I have given you so often before; and in the power of the judge to punish law-breakers, you will see another example of work done by all for the good of all.

Why We Should Honour the Judge.

6. For the judge is really appointed by the people to do their work for them, and it is only because he is acting for all the people that he has any right to sentence and to punish.

7. When you understand this, you will understand why it is that everyone is bound to respect and to honour those who are chosen as judges, and why we should all support and help those whose business it is to carry out the law.

8. As you learnt in Chapter VII, no one has a right to take the law into his own hands. It is only when a man acts on behalf of all his countrymen that he has a right to do such a solemn thing as to condemn his fellow-men to death, to send them to gaol, or even to take them prisoners in the street.

The Policeman.

9. And this is true not only of the judges on the bench, but it is true of every single man who helps to do the work of justice. You know that a policeman has the right to take up people who are disorderly in the streets, or who are seen stealing or fighting, and that he may do a great many other things which you and I have no right to do.

10. Why is this? What is the difference between the policeman

and any other man? The difference is that the policeman has been appointed, just as the judge has been appointed, to do his work for the whole people of the country. If the people had not given him his authority, he would have had no more business than you or I have to lock up or interfere with others. But because he is thus, in a small way, doing his work in the cause of law and justice, we ought to respect his office, and to help him in his work, remembering that without law and justice, we should be no better off than the worst savages.

Special Constables.

11. To show you how true it is that the work which the policeman does is really done on behalf of all the people who have given him his authority, I will tell you what happens when the policemen are too few for the work which they have to do, or when the dangers which they have to meet in order to protect the public are very great.

12. At such times, the plan is followed of "swearing-in special constables," that is to say, of appointing ordinary citizens to help the police. When special constables have been appointed, they too have the right to arrest people and to help to keep order just like policemen. It is usually in times of riot or great disturbance that they are appointed, and I have only spoken of them to show how really a policeman is doing work for you, and for me, and for all of us, which we should have to do for ourselves if he were not there.

CHAPTER IX.

THE NAVY AND ARMY—PART I.

"The blood of man should never be shed but to redeem the
blood of man. It is well shed for our family, for our
friends, for our God, for our country, for our kind—the
rest is vanity; the rest is crime."—*Edmund Burke.*

XXI.
The Defence of the Country.

1. ALL of you know something about our sailors and soldiers; you
know that their business is to protect the country at home and to
fight for it abroad. It would never do for me to tell you about the
duties of a British citizen and to say nothing at all about those who
are specially bound to fight for the country. For really, the duty of a
sailor or a soldier is the duty of every man in the whole Empire. It is
more convenient that during peace, only a few should give up their
time and their thought to making the country safe in time of war.

2. But we must never forget that the time might come when every
man, rich and poor, high and low, might have to become a sailor or a
soldier, and to risk his life for the defence of the country. If we were
attacked by any other nation, or there were a danger of our homes
being invaded and our liberty interfered with, then the time would
have come for every man, who was strong enough to carry a rifle,
to join the navy or the army, and to give up his time and his money,
and, if necessary, his life, in order that the enemy might be defeated.

Who Ought to Fight for the Country

3. You will see further on that by the law of the land, everybody is obliged to fight for the country if it is in danger. But luckily, there is not much need of a law to make British citizens do this; we may be sure that when the time comes, if it ever does come, we shall have plenty of defenders who will come forward, not because the law compels them, but because they love their country.

4. But, as you know, in times when there is no great danger, it is not necessary for everyone to become a soldier or a sailor. Only those who specially choose to go to sea or to join the army do so. When war comes, they are ready to fight for us, and when our rights are threatened in any part of the world, they are ready to go and see that justice is done, and, if necessary, to compel those who refuse us our rights to treat us justly.

Voluntary Enlistment and Conscription

5. I said that only those persons became sailors and soldiers who wished to do so, and happily, with us, that is so. In many countries, however, it is otherwise.

6. In France, in Germany, in Russia, in Austria, and in Italy, every man is compelled to become a soldier or a sailor whether he likes it or not, and is made to serve upon a ship of war or in a regiment for three or four years. This plan of making everybody a soldier or sailor is called conscription. In England, as you know, and in all the British Empire, there is no such thing, and our navy and army are recruited by voluntary enlistment, that is to say, they are made up only of those who wish to join them.

The Frontier of England

7. It is a great cause for thankfulness that we are able to be safe without a conscription, and we owe our good fortune chiefly to England being an island, and to all parts of her Empire being

THE FRONTIER OF ENGLAND.
(Dover Chiffs.)

separated from Europe. By being thus separated, we are not like most foreign nations afraid of sudden attack, for no enemy can cross our boundaries save by crossing the sea.

8. It would amuse you to see some of those places in Europe where the division between two countries runs. By just crossing the road, you can go from Germany into France, or from Austria into Germany, and you would never be any the wiser until you found out that you had changed from one set of laws, one language, and one government to another.

9. You see here two pictures. One of them shows you what the frontier line of our own country is like. It is a picture of the famous white cliffs of Dover, which look down upon the stormy waters of the British Channel, dividing us from France and from the whole of Europe by twenty miles of ever-changing water. It is of our ocean boundary that Shakespeare speaks in

the well-known lines in which he describes the ancient glories of England: -

> "This precious stone set in the silver sea,
> Which serves it in the office of a wall,
> Or as a moat defensive to a house,
> Against the envy of less happier lands;
> This blessed plot, this earth, this realm, this England."
>
> *Richard II., Act ii. Scene 1.*

Such is the advantage to us of being "bound in by the triumphant sea."

Another Frontier

10. And now look at the other picture, the little pillar with the word "Italia" written upon it. That is one of the boundary marks between Switzerland and Italy. On one side of the post you are in the Republic of Switzerland, land-governed by Swiss law; on the other side, you are in the Kingdom of Italy, liable, if you are living in the country, to be made to serve as a soldier in the Italian army at Rome, at Naples, or Turin, and governed by laws made at Rome instead of at Berne.

So you see we have a good deal to be thankful for in having a frontier which no one can mistake, and which no one can cross without our having full warning.

FRONTIER BETWEEN ITALY AND SWITZERLAND
(Boundary Post on the Simplon Pass.)

XXII.
Why the Navy Comes First

1. You will notice that I have spoken in this chapter of the "Navy and Army," and perhaps some of you will wonder why I did not talk of the army and navy, as people very often do. But, though it sounds a little strange to put the navy first, it is quite right. For the navy really ranks first, and if you were to be at a review where both sailors and soldiers were present, you would see that the sailors marched past before the soldiers.

2. Not very long ago, the Queen had a great review of volunteers at Windsor, and more than 30,000 men passed before her. But the very first to go past were the naval volunteers in their broad straw hats and white shirts. This is really as it ought to be, for after all, it is the sea which is our great defence, and it is those who protect our interests on the sea who ought to take the first place. The navy is the first line of defence; that is to say, it is not till the navy has been beaten that our shores can be invaded by an enemy. And thus it comes about that the navy is called the "Senior service."

Our Sailors

3. Let me therefore tell you something about our sailors, and the ships which they sail in. In the whole fleet, there are three or four hundred steamers and ships used for purposes of war, and furnished with guns of different sizes. Formerly, all ships were made of wood, and depended upon their sails only for getting from place to place.

4. Now, nearly all men-of-war are built of iron or steel, and some of them are protected from the enemies' shot by very thick plates of iron or steel placed upon their sides. These are called "ironclads." All of these vessels, large or small, are now steamers, and by means of their

H.M.S. "VICTORIA"

A BLUE-JACKET.

engines can go where they please, quite independently of the winds or the waves.

5. At the head of the fleet is an Admiral, and under him are Vice-Admirals and Rear-Admirals. Each ship is commanded by a captain, and under him are lieutenants, engineers, surgeons, boatswains, gunners, carpenters, and a great number of other officers, each charged with special duties.

SAILORS AT GUN DRILL.

The crew of each ship is made up of sailors, who are sometimes called blue-jackets, and of engineers and stokers to look after the machinery.

The Marines

6. Nor must I forget to mention the marines. On every ship, there are a certain number of men who belong to the Royal Marines. These men are trained like soldiers, but they go to sea in ships like sailors, and when it is necessary, they are landed from the ships to fight on land. The Royal Marines, though not exactly belonging either to the navy or the army, have fought bravely for our country in every part of the world, and have become justly famous.

7. Most of the blue-jackets go into the navy when they are quite boys, and this is a good plan, for to be a good sailor, it is necessary to be accustomed to the sea all one's life. The officers in the navy also join it when they are boys, and before they can be advanced from one rank to another, they are examined in order to see that they know their work well, for it is most important that those who take charge

of a great ship among all the dangers of the ocean should be ready to do the right thing at the right time, and be prepared for the many sudden accidents that may befall from storms or from the enemy.

What the Navy Does

The ships for the navy are chiefly built in the four great dock-yards—Portsmouth, Plymouth, Chatham, and Pembroke. When they are all ready, they are sent to sea. Some watch the coasts of Great Britain, others go across the ocean to protect our countrymen in Canada, in Australia, in New Zealand, and in all those other parts of the world where the Union Jack flies.

9. Others, again, are sent to take care of the many thousands of merchant ships which all the year round are crossing the sea, bringing corn and wool and a hundred other things to this country, or taking iron and coal and cloth from our mines and our mills to countries beyond the sea.

10. Some keep a look-out upon the slave ships, and others are employed in measuring the depth of the sea, in finding out the shape of unknown bays and peninsulas, and in correcting the maps which are contained in your atlases. Our sailors have much to do in time of peace; in time of war, we depend upon them for the safety of our lives and the freedom of our country.

11. The history of the Navy of England has been a very glorious one. Perhaps what has helped more than anything else to make it so is the fact that our greatest sailors, whether officers or seamen, have always made their chief thought the performance of their duty. "Duty" has been the great watchword of the navy, and it was because he knew how great a power this simple word would have over the minds of his men that Admiral Nelson chose for his message to the fleet at the great victory of Trafalgar, the famous words—"England expects every man to do his duty."

CHAPTER X.

THE NAVY AND ARMY—PART II

"Soldiers, your labours, your privations, your sufferings, and
your valour, will not be forgotten by a grateful country."—*From Sir Henry Havelock's Address to his Troops.*

XXIII.
The Army

1. And now I come to the army. The history of the British Army,
like that of the navy, is a very famous one, and many a book has been
written telling of the brave things which have been done by it. But
what I have got to do here is not to give you the history of the army,
but only to tell you how it is made up, and what it has got to do.

Artillery—Cavalry—Infantry—Engineers

2. The army is divided into four branches—the artillery, the
cavalry, the infantry, and the engineers. The artillery is composed of
different batteries, the cavalry and infantry of regiments, the engineers
of troops and companies. Besides these chief divisions, there are also
doctors and hospital attendants to look after the sick and wounded,
and a transport corps, a body of men whose business it is to carry
provisions and stores of all kinds for the soldiers who are fighting.

3. The artillery have cannon, some drawn by four, and some by
six horses.

The cavalry are armed with swords or lances, and being mounted
on horseback, are able to move quickly from place to place, to get

AN ARTILLERYMAN.

news, and to prevent the army from being surprised. The engineers have a great deal of work to do; they make bridges, build forts, lay down telegraph wires, and do many other things which nowadays are necessary in time of war.

4. The infantry are armed with rifles and bayonets, and are sepa-

A CAVALRY SOLDIER

rated into different regiments, each of which has the name of some part of the country; for instance, the Royal Sussex Regiment, the Sutherland and Argyll Highlanders, the Connaught Rangers, the Welsh Borderers, and the Canadian Fusileers. Each regiment is proud

AN INFANTRY SOLDIER.

of its history, and officers and men strive to make their own regiments excel all others in acts of bravery, in endurance, and in skill in arms.

5. At the head of each regiment, there is a colonel, and above

the colonels, there are generals, and above them again is the Commander-in-Chief.

Who Commands the Army and Navy

6. In name, the Queen is at the head of both the navy and army, but, as you may suppose, she does not take any active part in ordering them about or leading them. Still, it must be remembered that "the Crown" (as the King or Queen is sometimes called) is really the chief of both services.

7. But of course, there would be neither soldiers nor sailors if there were no money to pay them with, and money can only be got, as I told you, by taxes voted by the House of Commons. So, however much the Crown wanted to use the fleet or the army without consulting the whole people, it could not do it, because Parliament could refuse to vote the money to pay the sailors and soldiers.

8. I have told you this about the Queen, the Parliament, and the army because, though it is not very important nowadays, there was a time when there was a real danger of the king using the army to put down the people or to do things which were unjust and contrary to law. Fortunately, it is certain that our present Queen would not ever try to act contrary to law; but you will see that if ever, at any time, a king or queen of England should try to do so, the people have a way by which they can protect themselves.

Discipline

9. In some matters, British citizens who are in the navy or army are under different laws from those who belong to neither. It has been found that no army and no fleet can be well governed and directed unless there is strict discipline kept among all those in it. You know what discipline is, do you not? It is

the habit of obedience to orders given by those who have the right to give them. It is the habit of acting according to rules laid down and practiced beforehand, and of working together with others in such a way that there may be no confusion or dispute.

10. When boys and girls go out of school in order, one by one, class by class, they show that they have learned the use of discipline. When they do their drill, moving their hands or their feet together at the word of command, they show that they have learned the use of discipline.

11. There are very few things in the world which we should not do better for a little discipline, for practice, patience, faith in others, and obedience to just orders, which are the things that go to make up discipline, are useful in all that we have to do.

12. But in the army and navy above all, it is necessary that discipline should be absolute and strict, not because the good qualities I have told you of are more necessary to a soldier or a sailor than they are to any other man, but because in the dangers and difficulties of war, the consequences of being without any of them would be so terribly serious. I will give you some examples of the use of discipline in time of war.

Practice

13. In the great war with France in the reign of Edward III, the English archers were over and over again victorious. And what was the reason? Simply that every boy, as he grew up, was made to fire at a mark with a long bow until he became a good archer. When the time of battle came, he won because he had practice; the enemy were beaten because they had neglected to practice.

Patience

AN ENGLISH ARCHER.

14. To give you an example of the value of *patience* as a part of discipline, I cannot do better than to tell you the story of how Admiral Nelson watched the French fleet. It was in the year 1805 when the French, under Napoleon Buonaparte, had won a great many victories on land, and having conquered nearly all the other

LORD NELSON.
(From, a Miniature.)

nations of Europe, were trying to invade and conquer England. The French fleet at that time was in the harbour of Toulon in the south of France, and it was most important that it should not be allowed to escape and join Buonaparte[6], who was waiting for it with his army just opposite Dover. For months and months, through all the storms of winter, Admiral Nelson lay in wait off the mouth of Toulon harbour, watching the enemy as a cat watches a mouse.

15. It was a weary task, but Nelson was equal to it. As Southey, who wrote his life, truly says, "The patience with which he watched Toulon was an example of perseverance at sea which had never been surpassed." From May 1803 to August 1805, two years and five months in all, he went out of his ship but three times, each of these times was upon the King's service, and on no occasion did his absence exceed one hour. Encouraged by so good an example, the men on board the Admiral's ship were as determined and as patient as their commander, and at last, the reward came. The French fleet escaped, it is true, but Nelson followed them. He chased them across the Atlantic to the West Indies and back.

6   Napoleon Bonaparte was originally born Napoleone di Buonaparte. He later changed his name to the more French-sounding "Napoléon Bonaparte"

16. When he returned to Portsmouth after his long pursuit, he feared, after all, that the enemy had escaped him, for he could get no news of them. But he was not long in starting off after them. He found them at last off the coast of Spain, and on the 21st of October 1805, he fought the great battle of Trafalgar, in which he totally defeated the French and Spanish fleets and took away the last fear of invasion. As you know, he lost his life in the moment of victory, but he has left behind him the lesson of how great is the need of patience as a part of discipline, and how great results may be won by patient waiting no less than by courage and readiness in attack.

XXIV.
Faith in Others

1. When the battle of Inkerman in the Crimean War was fought, our troops were surrounded by a thick mist, and while they were thus shrouded in darkness, they were attacked by many thousands of the Russians. No man could see what his neighbors were doing; it was impossible to tell whether on the right or the left the enemy had not got the victory; there was only one thing to be done, namely, for each man to do the best he could, trusting that every one of his comrades would do the same.

2. This is what our soldiers did. Their orders were to stop and fight, and each of them carried out his orders. They *had faith* in others, and in each other, and in the end, the battle of Inkerman was won.

Obedience to Lawful Orders

3. Not very long ago, a British ship-of-war, the *Megara*, was overtaken in a storm and greatly injured. The water began to pour into her, and it was plain that unless she could be run on shore, she must sink, and those on board lose their lives. There was only one

way of running the ship on shore, and that was for the engineers and stokers to remain in the engine-room far below the water and to keep the engines going full speed. It was probable, almost certain, that when the ship struck the shore, she would fall over on her side, and that none but those on deck would escape with their lives.

4. But the engineers and stokers had orders to keep the fires burning and the engines working, and to obey their orders, they must stay below and run the risk of a terrible death. They did stay below, and at last, the sinking ship was run full speed onto the shore.

5. Mercifully, she remained stuck fast, and not only those on deck, but the brave men down below, were able to escape. But it was to their efforts that the whole crew owed their preservation; they had saved the ship because they had obeyed orders. You will see from these examples how great is the need for discipline in the army and navy.

The Value of Discipline

6. It is indeed so great that special rules and laws are made to punish those who disobey orders, who neglect their duty, or who are guilty of cowardice or misconduct in time of war.

7. These special rules are called "Martial Law," and though it seems hard at first that a man should be severely punished for doing that which, if he were not a soldier or a sailor, he would not be punished for at all, you will soon see that it is just, as well as necessary. For suppose a soldier were to refuse to obey his sergeant because he thought that he knew better what ought to be done, then why should not the sergeant in his turn refuse to obey his captain, the captain his colonel, and so on? Plainly, at that rate, each man would be going his own way, and the enemy would have very little trouble in sending such a disorderly army to the right-about.

8. Or again, suppose a soldier were to fall asleep at his post while he was keeping watch as a sentinel. Falling asleep is not wrong in itself, but think what may be the consequences. Over and over

again, great armies have suffered defeat, ships have been taken, and thousands have lost their lives because those whose duty it was to watch against surprise neglected their charge. For the safety of all, therefore, it is right that the man who falls asleep at his post should be punished in the severest manner.

9. And lastly, if a sailor or soldier proves himself a coward before the enemy, it is right that he should be punished at once and severely. For if one man is allowed to set the bad example of trying to save himself by giving way to his fears, then we may be sure that others will be moved by his bad example, or discouraged by his flight, and that a great advantage will be given to the enemy. So when we come to consider the consequences of these things, we shall understand why it is that it is right to punish under martial law.

10. But what is true for one man who is a soldier or a sailor is true for another. The sergeant will make the private soldier obey him, but if he wants him to do so, he must in his turn be ready to obey the captain, who gives him orders; and the captain, in his turn, must make his own wishes respected, but he must himself be a pattern of obedience to his superiors.

11. And so on, from rank to rank, from the highest to the lowest. There can be no shame in accepting orders from those who have themselves learned to obey, and you may be sure that if ever you hear a sailor or a soldier speak ill of discipline and complain of having to obey orders, that he is a black sheep, and that he will do very little credit to his ship or to his regiment.

The Loss of the "Birkenhead"

12. Before I finish this long chapter, I will give you one more story which will show you how noble a thing discipline may become. It is another story of the sea, only this time the heroes of the tale are soldiers and not sailors.

13. A great ship, the *Birkenhead*, was sailing along the coast of

Africa. On board of her were a number of soldiers, and besides the soldiers, there were many women and children. Suddenly the ship struck on a rock, and the water began to pour into her so fast that at last it became clear that in spite of all the efforts of the crew, she must soon sink. No help was in sight, and the only way of escape was by the boats, but the boats were too few to carry the whole number of those who were now crowded on the deck of the unhappy ship. Who was to go? The strong men who could try to save themselves, or the weak women and weaker children who were at their mercy?

14. To the credit of the British Army, there was no hesitation. The officer commanding the soldiers gave them the order to fall in upon the deck, just as they had often done before in the barrack yard. There, in order, they stood, while the sailors of the ship helped the women and children into the boats. Not a man broke from the ranks, not a man complained, the power of discipline was felt even in that terrible moment, and when at last the shattered ship sank into the dark waters, the red-coated English soldiers who went down with her had won a victory, as glorious as any that has ever been won on the hardest-fought battlefield.

15. One thing remains for me to tell you about the loss of the *Birkenhead*. King William of Prussia, who afterwards became Emperor of Germany, heard the story. He thought rightly that no better lesson of the true value of discipline to a soldier could well be given. The story was translated into German, and by the order of the King, it was read aloud to the soldiers at the head of every regiment in the Prussian army.

CHAPTER XI

THE AUXILIARY FORCES

"Defence not Defiance." – Motto of the Volunteers.

XXV.
Who are the Auxiliary Forces

1. WHAT is the meaning of "Auxiliary Forces"? Auxiliary forces mean those which are ready in time of need to come to the aid of the army and navy, or the "regular forces," as they are often called. You have perhaps not often heard of the auxiliary forces, but you have nearly all of you heard of the militia, the yeomanry, and the volunteers, and it is these that are meant by the words at the head of this chapter, for it is they who in time of need will come to the aid of the sailors and soldiers about whom I told you in the last chapter.

2. The Militia, like the army, are divided into artillery, infantry, and engineers, but there are no cavalry belonging to it. The men who join the militia do so for a certain length of time only, and have to serve as soldiers for two or three months during the year. While they are serving in the ranks, they receive pay like regular soldiers, but not at other times. When the two or three months are over, they go back to their homes till the next year.

3. If, however, the country is in great danger, and there is a threat of war, or if there is actually war going on, all the men in the militia are called out and are kept together in their regiments until there is no longer any need for their services. By law, the militia cannot be made to go and fight abroad, but over and over again, when there has

been a danger of war, many of the officers and men have volunteered of their own accord to go if required outside these islands to fight their country's battles.

Every man must serve if required.

4. I must not forget to tell you that though at present only those join the militia who wish to do so, yet there is a law, which, though it has not been used for a long time, still exists, by which all able-bodied men can be made to join it for the defence of the country. If Parliament thinks it necessary at any time, every man who is fit to bear arms may be called upon to serve in the militia, and he may be made to do so for as long a time as is necessary. This is called the "Ballot for the Militia," and is what I meant when I told you that by law every man might be made to serve his country as a soldier.

The Yeomanry

5. The yeomanry are quite different from the militia. In the first place, they are cavalry, that is to say, they are mounted on horses. They are generally farmers and those who know the country well and are good riders. They join of their own free will and serve for only a very short time during the year—often not more than a week.

The Volunteers

6. Most of you know something about the volunteers. In nearly every town and village, there is a corps of volunteers, either infantry, artillery, or engineers. In a few places, also, are to be found mounted volunteers, and in some of the sea-port towns, there are naval volunteers, or sailors.

7. The volunteers are all men who are ready to fight for the defence of the country if it is ever invaded, and who, in order to become useful soldiers, able to be of real service, are willing to give up a portion of their time and their attention to learning how to drill, to shoot,

and to do other things which a soldier must learn nowadays before he can be much good.

8. The first volunteer corps were formed in the year 1860, when there was some fear that we should be invaded by the French. The motto which was then taken by the new army of citizen soldiers is one which was well chosen, and which is still a very good one for every volunteer to bear in mind.

9. The motto was "*Defence not Defiance!*" that is to say, it is the duty of the volunteer to defend his country when attacked, but not to threaten the safety of any other country which does not interfere with us.

10. This is all that we ought to want, for as long as other nations will leave us alone, we can never want to defy them, or to do anything which might bring upon us or them the fearful suffering of a war.

The Use of the Volunteers

11. The volunteers are a great help to us in furnishing us with soldiers who will be able to defend us in time of need; and in time of peace, it is a good thing that rifle corps should be formed and kept up. In the first place, it is right that every man should feel that he owes something to the country which protects him by its laws, and which gives him the freedom which he enjoys, and that he should be ready to give up some time and some care to do it a service. In the second place, it is a good thing to have a means whereby men, and young men especially, can learn how discipline depends upon obedience, and how good order and useful work depend upon both.

XXVI.
Our Countrymen in the Colonies

1. But before I close this chapter, I must ask you to look once again at the map at the beginning of this book, and to count up once more the number of places marked red, which, as I told you, are the

places where the Union Jack flies, and where our fellow-countrymen live and work.

2. There is not a corner of the world where you will not see the red colour.

3. In British Columbia in the North, in the great Australian continent, and in the little Falkland Islands, far down in the South; at Hong Kong in the East, and in Canada and Jamaica in the West, you will find it. And when you see how far it spreads, and how great a part of the earth it covers, you may well ask: How can all these colonies and possessions, great and small, be preserved and protected by the army and navy of the little islands which make up the United Kingdom?

4. Certainly, if we had no help, the work could not be done. It would be too great for us with all our strength and with all our wealth. But fortunately, we are not left to do the work alone. Our countrymen, though they live far across the sea, have not so changed from what their ancestors were at home, that they are not ready and able to fight in their own defence and for their own rights.

5. In Canada, in Australia, and in New Zealand, there are men trained to the use of arms and to the handling of ships of war; and there can be no doubt that if any of these great colonies were to be attacked by a foreign nation, they would not leave us to fight their battles alone, but would strike a blow in their own defence.

6. Nor is this all. It is only a short time ago since a proof was given that those who have left our shores and have gone to seek their fortunes in far-off colonies have not forgotten the country from which they sprang, and of whose greatness they are so proud. Not only have they not forgotten it, but they have shown clearly to all the world that they must be counted with by any nation which seeks to injure the Old Country.

How Australia helped the Old Country

7. I hope most of you will remember how not very long ago our countrymen in the great colony of New South Wales came forward of their own accord and sent their soldiers to fight side by side with our own redcoats in Africa. Not only did they send their soldiers to share our dangers, but they paid the whole cost of providing them with arms and uniforms, of carrying them in steamers across the sea, of paying the officers and men as long as they were wanted, and of giving help to their relations at home in case those in the field were hurt.

8. It was a great day for you and me and all of us who belong to this great empire when the men of New South Wales came to fight shoulder to shoulder with our soldiers from London, from Edinburgh, and from Dublin. It is to be hoped that if ever a real danger threatens our land, not only the men of New South Wales, but the men of Victoria, of Canada, of New Zealand, and all our other colonies will be ready to help us. I believe they will be ready.

9. But the knowledge that we have so many and such powerful friends ought not to make us more ready to use our strength. On the contrary, we ought rather to be ten times more careful to avoid a quarrel than we are now, for we must remember that we have not only ourselves to think of, but that we have to consider the millions of our countrymen all over the world who may suffer from our mistakes, and who will rightly enough say that we have no business to make wars without asking them.

The Horrors of War

10. And before I finish these chapters upon our sailors and soldiers, whether they be those who belong to the regular Navy and Army, or whether they be Volunteers, I will say one thing which is true of all of them and of the work which they have to do.

11. The work of sailors and soldiers is to fight. And there are times when, as I have already told you, it is right and necessary

that they should do so. But we must never forget for a moment that war, even though it be justly undertaken, is one of the most fearful misfortunes which can befall a people. Happily, we in England know very little of the misery and the suffering which are the result of war.

12. We ought to be thankful that it is so, but we must remember that no war can ever be fought without causing pain, and sorrow, and ruin, and death to many, and that even worse than the outward misfortunes which war causes are the bad and cruel feelings, the hatred, the cruelty which it often gives rise to in the hearts of those who make it or take part in it.

13. I trust that none of you will ever see a battle-field, or visit a country just after it has been swept by war. If you are ever tempted to think that war is a glorious thing, or that fighting can ever be anything but horrible, try and learn from the accounts of those who have seen real war what its results always are and must be.

14. The dead and dying on the battle-field, the long trains of wounded, the hospitals with their scenes of agony, the ruined and blackened houses, the crops scattered, the fields uncultivated; and then again, far from the scene of battle, the relations and friends of those who have been fighting, sorrowing over the dear ones they have lost; and then, one step further still, picture to yourselves the poverty that is caused by trade being stopped, and business being interfered with, and by the hard-earned money of the people being spent upon the Army; and you will begin to understand what are some of the consequences of war.

Unjust Wars

15. And if all these things be true of a war which is necessary and just, how much more dreadful must be the consequences of entering upon a war which is neither necessary nor just? Then to

all the suffering and misery which I have described would be added the shame and guilt of having brought upon tens of thousands of innocent persons the consequences of our own folly and our own bad passion.

16. England in the past has not always been free from the charge of entering upon wars for bad reasons, for insufficient reasons, or without enough thought of the consequences. There is no more important duty which you, all of you, whether boys or girls, will have to perform as British citizens when you grow up, than to keep this country from entering upon unjust or unnecessary wars.

17. The decision between peace and war will rest with you, for nowadays we cannot say, as in the old times, that England is driven into war by kings, by the nobles, or by any small number of people. The whole people now have the right to say whether there shall be war or not. And if England ever makes war unjustly, the blame of it will henceforward lie upon the shoulders of every citizen who has not done his or her best to prevent it.

CHAPTER XII.

THE FLAG – PART I.

"Here and here did England help me: how can
I help England?" - Browning.

XXVII.
The Union Jack.

1. I HOPE you all know the "Union Jack," the flag of England; at any rate, here is a picture of it, which will tell you what it is like. After all, perhaps some of you will say, what is the use of giving us a lesson about the Union Jack, what can there be to tell about that we do not know?

2. We know that it is a pretty pattern, made of pieces of cloth sewn together; we know that it is used for decorating the streets when there are processions, and it is carried by soldiers and sailors in battle. Now all these things are true, but they are not the whole truth, for there is, indeed, a great deal more to be said about the Union Jack than this. In the first place, how do we come to have a flag at all, and what is the meaning of it?

3. The flag is now the outward sign of the authority of the English people. In itself, it is true, it is only a piece of silk or bunting[7], but really it is more than this, for it is known to all the world that it is the sign which the English people have chosen to distinguish them

7   Bunting, the material large flags are made of.

and their possessions all over the world, and to show to other nations where England claims to govern and to be obeyed.

A LIST OF THE VARIOUS COUNTRIES, ISLANDS, TERRI-TORIES AND POSSESSIONS WHICH MAKE UP THE "BRITISH EMPIRE" AND IN WHICH THE "UNION JACK" FLIES: -

THE BRITISH ISLANDS— ....*Population*

England and Wales -	27,974,000
Scotland -	3,735,000
Ireland -	5,174,000
The Isle of Man -	54,000
The Channel Islands -	90,000

THE UNION JACK.

Great Countries chiefly inhabited by Englishmen:
NORTH AMERICA—

    Canada - 5,000,000
    Newfoundland -... 193,000

AUSTRALASIA—

    New South Wales -.. 1,003,000
    Victoria -... 1,009,000
    New Zealand -... 578,000
    Queensland - 309,000
    South Australia - 313,000
    Western Australia -.. 35,000
    Tasmania - 133,000

Places colonized by Englishmen, but in which those of English descent are outnumbered by natives, or those of some other race -
SOUTH AFRICA - Cape Colony -.................................1,240,000
                    Natal -..424,000
                    Griqualand West –.............................50,000
                    Bechuanaland -.......................*Not ascertained*
                    Zululand -............................... *Not ascertained*
                    Walfisch Bay - ....*Not ascertained*

NOTE.—In the South African Colonies there are a large number of persons of Dutch descent as well as the natives.
WEST AFRICA -   Gambia –...14,000
                    Gold Coast and Lagos – 450,000
                    Sierra Leone – 60,000

ASIA –   Straits Settlements – 500,000
SOUTH AMERICA – British Guiana –...............................260,000
                    British Honduras – 28,000

Islands forming part of the Empire and colonized by men of English race, but in which there is still a large number of natives, or persons not of English race –

Bahamas (West Indies) – 45,000
Barbados (North Atlantic) –............................. 171,000
Ceylon (Indian Ocean) – 2,825,000
Fiji Islands (Pacific Ocean) – 121,000
Jamaica and Turk's Island (West Indies) – 585,000
Labuan (China Seas) – 6,000
Leeward Islands (West Indies) –........................... 120,000
Mauritius (Indian Ocean) – 370,000
New Guinea (East Indies) – .... *Not ascertained*
Trinidad (West Indies) –....................................... 153,000
Windward Islands (West Indies) including –
    Grenada – 46,000
    St. Lucia –..43,000
    St. Vincent – 42,000
    Tobago – 18,000

Places and Islands kept partly for commercial purposes, but chiefly as military ports to protect the Empire –

MEDITERRANEAN—   Gibraltar.—................... 24,000
    Malta – 157,000
    Cyprus – 186,000

RED SEA—   Aden –...................................... }
    Perim –..................................... } 40,000

CHINA SEAS—   Hong Kong –........................... 180,000
NORTH ATLANTIC- Bermuda –................................ 14,000
SOUTH ATLANTIC— Ascension –...................................... 400
    St. Helena –................................. 6,000

Possessions under the Governor-General of India, peopled by a
number of natives, and under the Government of a few Englishmen -

<pre>
India ....⎫
Burmah⁸ ....⎬ 240,000,000
                                                       ⎭
</pre>

Countries under the protection of the British Empire—Zanzibar
and the parts of Africa outlined on the map.

4. It is not perhaps very easy to understand what I have just told
you, until you come to some examples which I will give you of the
use of the flag, and the purposes which it ought rightly to serve.

What the Union Jack means.

5. But first, I think it will amuse you to know how it came about
that the Union Jack became the flag of England at all, and why it
is that it is made up of the different patterns which you see in the
picture. Let us take the pattern to pieces and put it together again. If
you look carefully, you will see that the flag is made up of a number
of different crosses, some red and some white. Now each of these
crosses has a meaning and a history.

6. First there is a large red cross in the middle, which is shaped
thus + and which has a white border round it, that is called the cross
of St. George, and is the sign of England. If any of you are fortunate
enough to have a new sovereign, you will see on it a picture of St.
George killing the dragon, as is told in the old legend. From very
early times, St. George has been called the Patron Saint of England,
and that is why the St. George's cross is used upon the Union Jack
to mark the place of England.

7. Then, if you look again, you will see that there is a white
cross shaped like this X upon a blue ground. That, according to
the old legend, is the cross of St. Andrew, and was for long the sign

8   Upper Burmah, of which the population is not yet exactly known, was
annexed to the British Empire in 1886.

of Scotland. And lastly, you will see that there is another cross of the same shape as the last, only red upon a white ground, and that is the cross of St. Patrick, the great Saint of Ireland and so the three crosses have a meaning, and what they mean is the union of England, Scotland, and Ireland.

8. It was in the reign of George III., in the year 1801[9], that the idea of joining together the crosses of the three countries was first put into practice, to mark the union of the three countries. Since that time, the Union Jack has been the national flag, and has been carried to every corner of the world.

The Use of the Flag.

9. Now I have told you what the pattern on the Union Jack means, I must go back to what I said at the beginning of the chapter and explain to you what it is used for and what is the good of it.

10. You know that you often hear of flags carried by soldiers in battle, and by warships on the sea, but though the Union Jack has been carried by British soldiers and sailors in many a hard fight, you must not suppose that it has not any use in time of peace. Quite the contrary; indeed, some of the most useful purposes which our flag is made to serve have nothing whatever to do with wars and fighting.

11. In short, when the Union Jack is properly used in any place, it is as much as to say, "Here is something belonging to England, and which the people of England have undertaken to protect." It may be placed upon a fortress, or a ship of war, or it may be placed over the house in which an English Ambassador lives in a foreign country, while sometimes it is hoisted in a country which has not ever had a civilised government, and then all the world knows that from that time forward England is going to undertake the government of that country, and to see that right and justice are done there.

9   The Union with Ireland was in 1800.

KHARTOUM AND THE NILE.

12. When the flag is pulled down, or taken away, then it is known that our country has no longer the will or the power to have its wishes obeyed in the place from which the flag has gone.

XXVIII.
The Story of Khartoum.

1. So it was at Khartoum when Sir Charles Wilson, with his little band of sailors and soldiers, came too late to rescue General Gordon and his brave garrison from the Arabs who were besieging them. For hours, the two steamers made their way up the river, and at last, they got near to the besieged city; the enemy fired at them from both banks, and many of the party were wounded, but still, they pressed on, determined to save their countryman if he were still alive.

2. Soon all eyes were strained to see if the flag were still waving over the house where Gordon had lived so long, and which he had defended so bravely. Alas, they looked in vain! The flag was not there, and then they knew that they were indeed too late, that the day was lost, and that Khartoum had fallen into the hands of the

GENERAL GORDON.

enemy. All this they learned in a moment, when they saw that the flag was no longer flying.

The Flag at Lucknow.

3. Happily, we have not always been too late, and I will tell you another story of danger and rescue, where the flag was still flying when the rescuers came.

4. It was at the famous siege of Lucknow, in India, during the terrible mutiny of the native soldiers against the English government, of which I have already told you something.

5. English men, women, and children, with a few faithful natives, were shut up in a large house called the Residency, and surrounded

by thousands of the enemy; they were exposed by day and night for nearly five months to the bullets of the enemy. Many were killed, many were wounded, and many fell sick under the terrible heat of the Indian sun.

6. Sir Henry Lawrence, the brave general in command, was killed by a cannon shot, but still, the little band of Englishmen refused to give in. At one time their hopes revived when General Havelock with a small number of English soldiers broke through the enemy and made his way into the Residency, but so great was the number of the besiegers that the rescuers found themselves shut up in their turn, and unable to get out. So passed three weary months till hope died away, and the end seemed near.

The Relief.

7. But help was at hand. Sir Colin Campbell, with 5,000 fresh soldiers, was advancing by forced marches to the relief of the besieged city.

8. Over and over again it seemed impossible that his little army could cut their way through the forces of the enemy now elated by their victories. But one great thought was always in the minds of every one of the rescuers, from the General downwards. The lives of Englishmen, and more than that, of English women and children, depended upon their success.

9. What would be the fate of their countrymen if they arrived too late? And so under the scorching sun, and under the bullets of the enemy, they pressed on, and as at last they came near to the city, the question rose to every man's lips, "Is it too late?"

10. Then as the distant walls and towers of Lucknow came in sight, they turned their eyes upon the one building still surrounded by the smoke of battle, and there above the Residency of Lucknow they beheld the flag of England still waving, and the flag told them from afar off that they were not too late; that their work was not in

THE RELIEF OF LUCKNOW.

vain, and that ere another day was passed, they might press to their hearts the loved ones who so long had stood upon the brink of death.

11. There is a great poem by Tennyson which tells the story of the Siege of Lucknow, and of the first relief by Sir Henry Havelock. I hope you will read it for yourselves, but one or two verses I will give you now. First, the poet describes the besieged fortress with the Union Jack still floating over the shattered walls of the Residency, and gives us a picture of the sufferings and dangers of the little garrison:—

12. Banner of England! Not for a season, O banner of Britain, hast thou

Floated in conquering battle or flapt to the battle-cry!
Never with mightier glory than when we had reared thee on high,
Flying at top of the roof, in the ghastly siege of Lucknow,
Shot thro' the staff or the halyard[10], but ever we raised thee anew,
And ever upon the topmost roof our banner of England blew.
Frail were the works that defended the hold that we held with our lives—
Women and children among us—God help them—our children and wives!
Hold it we might—and for fifteen days or for twenty at most.
"Never surrender, I charge you, but every man die at his post!"
Voice of the dead whom we loved—our Lawrence, the best of the brave,
Cold were his brows when we kissed him—we laid him that night in his grave.
"Every man die at his post!"—and there hailed on our homes and halls
Death from their rifle bullets, and death from their cannon balls;
Death in our innermost chamber, and death at our slight barricade;

10 Halyard, the rope for hauling up the flag on the staff.

Death while we stood with the musket, and death while we stooped to the spade;

Death to the dying, and wounds to the wounded—for often there fell,

Striking the hospital wall, crashing thro' it, their shot and their shell.

13. And the poem ends with the glad news of the relief, and the meeting of General Havelock's soldiers with the poor women and children whom they had come to rescue:—

Hark! Cannonade, fusillade! Is it true what was told by the scout?

Outram and Havelock breaking their way through the fell mutineers.

Surely the pibroch[11] of Europe is rising again in our ears!

All on a sudden the garrison utter a jubilant shout,

Havelock's glorious Highlanders answer with conquering cheers,

Sick from the hospital echo them, women and children come out,

Blessing the wholesome white faces of Havelock's good Fusileers,

Kissing the war-hardened hand of the Highlander wet with their tears;

Dance to the pibroch!—Saved! We are saved! Is it you! Is it you?

Saved by the valour of Havelock! Saved by the blessing of Heaven!

Hold it for fifteen days—We have held it for eighty-seven!

And ever aloft on the palace roof, the old banner of England flew.

14. I have told you these two stories, of failure and success, to show you how the flag plays the part of a sign and an emblem to the world. At Khartoum the flag was gone, and that meant that England had no longer any power there, for good or for evil. At Lucknow the flag still floated, and from it, men knew that the power of England was still upheld.

15. As to the story of Khartoum, or the story of Lucknow, they

11   Pibroch, the war song of the Scotch Highlanders.

are well worth reading in some books which tell you all about them at full length. They are splendid stories of bravery and endurance, which will make you all feel proud of being Englishmen.

I have told you about them quite shortly here, only to show you what I meant about the flag.

CHAPTER XIII.
THE FLAG. - PART II.

"A great Empire and little minds go ill together." – Burke

XXIX.
Peace.

1. BUT the Union Jack has its uses in time of peace as well as in time of war. Always remember that there is a great saying, which you will find repeated in your histories, "No slave can breathe under the flag of England."

2. What is the meaning of this saying? It means that as, by the law of England, no man can be a slave, so wherever the flag of England waves, everyone is and must be free.

3. It may seem strange that I should think this so important, for you may well ask who could think of making slaves of other men nowadays?

4. Fortunately, this is true indeed of England, and of all parts of the British Empire; but it was not always true, even of England and her colonies, and now at this moment there are still countries where the wicked practice of buying and selling men and women as slaves is still kept up.

The Flag and Slavery.

5. It is not much more than a hundred years ago, in 1772, that the judges decided that, by the law of England, no man could be a slave within the British islands, but though we were ashamed of slavery at

WILBERFORCE.

home, we still allowed our countrymen to practise it abroad.

6. At last, however, people in England began to understand how shameful it was that, in any part of the world, slavery should be allowed under the British flag, and first of all an effort was made by some of the best men in Parliament, the chief among whom was Wilberforce, to put an end to the slave-trade, that is to say, the buying or capturing of slaves in Africa, and carrying them across the ocean to the colonies in America and the West Indian Islands. After many fruitless attempts, and much disappointment, the friends of the slave at last got their own way, and Parliament did away, once and for all, with the slave-trade.

7. But to get rid of the slave-trade was not enough. It was true that our flag no longer waved over those horrible slave ships, but in countries where the Union Jack showed that England bore rule, slaves were still kept, and bought and sold, and made to labour like dumb animals. The work of Wilberforce was not completed, but fortunately, there were others, no less zealous in the good cause than he, who gave up their lives to persuading the people of England to do away with slavery everywhere throughout the world where Englishmen had the making of the law.

8. One great difficulty had to be got over: the owners of the slaves had bought them under the law, and until the law was changed, they had a legal right to keep them. It was thought just, therefore, to give to the slave-holders some payment in money, so that they might not all be ruined by the change in the law. At last, the people and the Parliament were persuaded, and, in the year 1833, an Act of Parliament was passed by which all the slaves throughout the British Empire were set free, and a payment of twenty million pounds was made to the former slave-owners.

9. Now, at last, England had her hands free, and could help others to get rid of the great evil which she had herself put away.

10. All civilised nations have agreed to put down the slave-trade, and whenever a slave-trader sees the British flag on a ship of war, he tries to escape, for he knows that the captain of the English ship has orders to take every slave ship that he sees, to set free the slaves, and to give up the trader to be punished.

Freedom under the Union Jack.

11. Not very long ago, some slaves on the African coast swam off to an English ship, and claimed to be free under the British flag. By some mistake, they were sent back to their masters; but when this was known in England, everyone was angry and indignant, and orders were given that such a thing should never be allowed to happen again. So now, whenever a slave can place himself under the shadow of the Union Jack, he knows that he will be free, and that no man will be allowed to claim him.

12. Then again, as I told you, the flag is used to show that some uninhabited or uncivilised[12] country has been taken in the name of the Queen for the people of England, and that from that time it is to become part of the British Empire. Look at the island on your

12   This reflects the colonial mindset of the time, which, unfortunately, often dismissed the presence, cultures, and governance of Indigenous peoples.

HOSTING THE UNION JACK IN NEW GUINEA.

map called New Guinea. There you will see a patch coloured red, which, as I told you, meant that it was part of the British Empire.

13. A few years ago, only that red patch would not have been there, for it was only in the year 1883 that a party of our country-men landed on the island and hoisted the Union Jack in the name of Queen Victoria.

Why We Should Honour the Flag.

14. I think I have told you enough to show you what the flag really is, and what is the use of it. What I particularly want you to remember is that the flag is nothing in itself; but because it stands before other people as the mark of our country, it means a great deal. It is right and useful that men should honour and love the flag, and be prepared to lose their lives in defending it, as many of our countrymen have done before now; but we must bear in mind that it is not really the piece of coloured silk that is worth fighting

for or dying for, but only the honour and reputation of the country which has chosen it for its own.

15. And so, as long as you do your best to make the British Empire the first among the nations in all that is right and just, so long will you do well to honour and to love the flag which, by the bravery and the wisdom of our forefathers, has become so famous.

CHAPTER XIV.

TAXATION.

"All for each and each for all."

XXX.
What Are Taxes?

1. IN the last few chapters, I have been telling you about all the different things that have to be done in order that the country may be well governed and protected. You have learnt how justice is done, how the Post Office, the Foreign Office, the Education Office, and all the other offices are worked.

2. Of course, it is quite plain that all these things cannot be done for nothing. The judges must be paid, the ships of war must be built, the postmen must receive their wages, and money must be provided for all the different purposes which I have described to you. How is this money to be got, who is to pay it, and how is it to be collected? Let us first consider for whose good the money is spent, and then we shall soon see who it is ought to pay it.

3. Formerly, a great part of what is now the country of Holland lay beneath the sea. Year by year, for many centuries, the Dutch have laboured to reclaim from the waves the land on which their towns are built, and the fields upon which they feed their cattle and grow their corn. To keep out the waters of the German Ocean, great embankments of earth and masonry, called dykes, have been built for miles along the coast. Outside the dykes is the sea. Inside and below the level of the sea are the fertile fields of Holland.

4. If once the dykes were to break, the water would come pouring in and would destroy in a few hours the work of many years' patient labour. If such a calamity were to happen, it is not the rich only or the poor only, it is not the farmer alone nor the manufacturer, but everybody, rich and poor, high and low, who would be overwhelmed by the rush of the waters. It is, therefore, necessary, for the protection of all, that the dykes should be kept up and in good repair. And as everybody alike is protected by the dykes, so everyone is called upon to pay for maintaining them.

What is maintained for the public good should be paid for out of the public money.

5. Not long ago, a very large building, known as the "Royal Courts of Justice," was built in London. Inside it are the Courts in which judges sit to try cases which are brought before them from

THE DYKES OF HOLLAND.

all parts of England. And besides the Courts, there are a very large number of offices, where those who are entrusted with the duty of administering justice and looking after the proper carrying out of the law, do their work. This great building cost no less than a million pounds, a very large sum, as you will allow, and far more than any single person could afford to pay.

Who Pays?

6. Now, who did pay this large sum? It is plain that if only those persons who used the Courts, those who went to law to get their own disputes settled by the judges, had to pay, they would very soon be ruined; and, indeed, they would never try to get justice done to them if it cost so dear. How then has the money been got? First of all, we must consider who it is uses the Courts, and who it is that goes to law. As a matter of fact, the number of people who really do go to law is not very large. But, though everyone does not use the Courts, everyone has the right to use them whenever he requires to do so.

7. The law exists for the benefit of all, rich and poor alike, and it is not only those who actually get their disputes settled before the judges who get the benefit of the law. As long as there are judges who will decide fairly, and Courts in which every man can get justice done to him, so long is the country safe from all the danger and discontent which always spring up where there is no true justice. And thus it is, that though everybody does not use the Royal Courts of Justice, yet everybody benefits by them.

8. And so, we come back to the question: who ought to pay for building the Courts? And the answer is that those who get the benefit of them ought to pay for them. But, as we have seen, everybody gets the benefit of them, and therefore, everybody ought to pay for them. And this is what really happens—public works are paid for out of public money.

9. From these two illustrations, I hope you will understand what

THE ROYAL COURTS OF JUSTICE.

I am going to tell you about taxes and taxation, and that you will learn how it is that the money is collected, not only for building the Law Courts, but for doing all the great public works of which I told you in the last few chapters.

What Taxes Are.

10. Taxes are *payments made by all for the good of all*. There are many things which must be done in a great country like England which cannot possibly be done by separate people, but which must be undertaken by the Government of the country for the benefit of all.

11. Thus, for instance, it is necessary, as I told you, that the judges should be paid, that the courts of law should be built, that the postmen should receive their wages, that our soldiers and sailors should get their pay, and that ships should be built. All these things are necessary for everybody alike. It is true that everybody does not go to law, but it is true, too, that if there were no judges, there would be no way of justly settling disputes, and no way of punishing wrongdoers, and we should find out very soon that a country in which there was neither law nor justice was one in which no man could live with safety and happiness.

12. So, too, with our soldiers and sailors. Everyone does not wish to go into the army or navy; very few people, it is to be hoped, wish the country to go to war for the sake of fighting only, but all of us, whatever our station in life, are made more secure because of the protection which the army and navy give to this country. And if you think for yourselves, you will find many other things which are done for the good of all, and which, therefore, ought to be paid for by all.

13. The money to pay for these things comes from the *taxes*. I will tell you a little further on what the taxes are and how they are collected.

You will see that all the objects which I have spoken about concern everybody in the kingdom, wherever they may live and whatever may be their occupation.

Rates.

14. You know that a great many things have to be done in every town and village for the comfort and convenience of those who live in it. The streets have to be repaired, the drains have to be made and kept in order, policemen have to be paid to preserve order and to take charge of criminals. Of course, every man in a town could not keep in order the streets through which he passed, nor would any one man be able, nor indeed be allowed, to pay a policeman for his own use only. So, for all these things, and many others, it is usual to follow the same plan as I told you was followed in the case of the judges, the postmen, the army, and the navy. The townsmen and villagers join together to pay for these things, which are necessary to all who live in the town or village. The payments which are made for these purposes are called *Rates*.

15. Of course, there is often a great difference between the things which are required in a large town and in a small village. In a large town, for instance, the danger of fire is much greater than it is in a village, where all the houses are apart from one another, and it is necessary, therefore, to provide fire-engines and firemen in the one case, which are not needed in the other.

16. And even between two large towns, there are often great differences; for instance, in a town on the sea-shore, such as Brighton, it is often necessary to have a strong wall to keep out the sea, whereas, in inland towns, such as Birmingham or Leeds, no sea wall is required.

17. For this reason, the collection of rates, unlike that of taxes, is left to the people of each town and village, and is not decided by Parliament. In the City of London, it is the Lord Mayor and

Corporation who fix the amount of the rates[13] and collect them. In that part of London which is outside the City, it is the vestries elected by those who pay the rates. In most towns, it is the Town Council, the members of which are also elected by the ratepayers, who perform this duty. In many towns, rates are levied for other purposes than those which I have mentioned. For instance, the lighting of the streets and the supply of water are paid for out of the rates.

18. In London, however, and in some other places, both gas and water are supplied by private companies, who provide the water and make the gas at their own expense, and sell them to those who require them. It is true that in London and elsewhere the payments which are made for gas and water are called *gas rates* and *water rates*, but they are not rates in the same sense as the other payments I have been speaking about, for they are not paid to a Town Council, or a vestry, or to any public body, but to private persons, who do the work which is required for the sake of making a profit. It is well to bear this distinction in mind when we talk of "the rates," and to remember to whom the payment really goes.

School Rates.

19. There is one other kind of rate which I must mention here, though you will find more about it in Chapter XVIII., and that is the School Board rate. This, like all other rates, is a payment made by all for the good of all. It is for the good of all that children should not be allowed to grow up in ignorance, and, therefore, it is the duty of all to see that proper means of education are supplied. The School

13   The rates collected by the County Councils mentioned on p. 53 are the rates required for a whole district or county. In London they are the rates required for the whole County of London. In Bedfordshire, for the whole County of Bedford; &c. The Town Council or Vestry collects rates for each town or division of a town: for instance, the Bedford Town Council collects rates to be spent in the town of Bedford; the Chelsea Vestry, rates to be spent in Chelsea only.

Board rate is fixed, not by the Town Council or Corporation, but by the School Board, which is a body elected on purpose to look after the education of children in any town or village.

XXXI.
What the Country Pays.

1. I will now give you one or two facts which will interest you about the quantity of money that is required in a single year for doing the work of the country.

2. You know how in every home there is so much money comes in and so much goes out. All the money that the father of the family or any other member of it earns, the profit made upon business or trade, and any other sums which are paid to those who live in the home, are incomings or income.

3. Everything that has to be paid away, such as rent, money for butchers' and grocers' bills, money for clothes, boots, and so on, make the outgoings or expenditure. If it be a wisely ordered household, care will always be taken that the incomings are more than the outgoings; and if it turns out that more has been spent than has been received, a wise man will at once set to work to see if he cannot give up some of the things that cost money, and do with a little less, so that at the end of the year he may have a little to the good, and have something to put into the bank instead of owing money to others.

4. So it is, or so it ought to be, with the country. On the one side there are the incomings, and on the other the outgoings, and it is always the duty of a good government and a wise parliament to spend less than is received.

The Country's Accounts.

5. For example, in a single year, 1883, the incomings or revenue of the country amounted to eighty-seven million pounds,

and the outgoings or expenditure to eighty-six million nine hundred and ninety-nine thousand pounds.

6. Out of the eighty-seven millions received, forty-six millions, or more than half, came from taxes on beer, spirits, tobacco, tea, and a few other things about which I will tell you further on. Nearly three millions were from taxes on houses and land, while between eight and nine millions were made up out of the shillings paid for telegrams, and the pennies, twopences, and threepences paid for postage stamps on letters.

7. Out of the eighty-six million nine hundred thousand spent, nearly twenty-nine million, or almost one-third of the whole, went to the navy and army for ships, guns, men, pensions, and uniforms. Six millions were spent on the law, for paying the judges, building law courts, and building and keeping up the prisons. Four million and a half were spent upon education. How is all this enormous amount of money to be collected, and who is to pay it? It is paid by the taxpayers, and is collected in two different ways.

Direct and Indirect Taxes.

8. Taxes, as I told you, are the payments made by everyone in proportion to his means, for the common good of the whole country. They are called *direct* and *indirect*. This seems at first rather a hard sentence to understand, but it is not so really; let me explain.

Direct Taxes.

9. Direct taxes are sums of money paid directly to the collectors sent round by the Government to take them. For instance, there is a tax which is called the income-tax. Everyone who receives more than £150 a year has to pay a tax, so much for every £100. The larger

the "income" a man receives, the larger is the sum he has to pay. The income-tax varies from about £1 10s. to £3 for every £100.

10. Again, those who own houses have to pay a tax for them. A tax must be paid for leave to keep a carriage, or to keep a dog, though it will perhaps amuse you to know that shepherds' dogs, who work as hard for their living as their masters do, are not taxed; nor are the dogs which blind men sometimes keep to lead them about the streets. This is quite right, for it is always wisest to tax only those things which people can do without if they choose, but which they keep for their own pleasure and enjoyment. In this way there is less chance of the taxes bearing too hard upon the very poor and those who are unable to pay them.

11. All these examples are given to show you what is the meaning of direct taxation.

PAYERS OF DIRECT TAXES.

Indirect Taxes.

12. Now I must say a word to you about *indirect* taxation, and what that means. I daresay a good many of you have paid indirect taxes yourselves without knowing it.

13. Every time you drink a cup of tea you are paying an *indirect tax*. Every time a man drinks a glass of beer or a glass of wine he is paying an *indirect tax*.

14. This seems rather strange at first sight, but it is quite true, as you will see when I have explained what I mean. As you know, all the tea that is drunk in this country comes to us from abroad. The tea-leaves which you buy at the grocer's shop are grown on bushes in China or India, and brought thence across the sea in ships.

15. As soon as the tea reaches this country, the merchant who brings it has to declare how much there is in each cargo, and for every pound of tea that is landed he has to pay fourpence as a tax to the Government. When I tell you that no less than 158,000,000 pounds weight of tea are sometimes landed in this country in a single year, you will see that the sum of money paid to the Government in this way must be very great indeed. And so it is. In the year 1883, no less than £4,200,000 was received in the way of taxes upon tea[14].

16. But tea is not the only thing which is taxed in this manner. Wine, beer, and spirits are all made to furnish part of the money which is required for the service of the country.

17. The taxes upon wine and spirits are very large, and this is quite right; for in the first place, it is always best to tax those things which are only used for enjoyment or pleasure, and which are not really necessary for the use of man; and in the second place, so much harm is done by the wrong use of wine and spirits, and drunkenness is so dreadful and horrible a thing, that, if anything at all is to be taxed,

14   The tax upon tea was lowered in 1890 from 6d. to 4d. per lb.

it is surely right that the strong drinks which are often the cause of so much misery should be chosen.

18. Besides tea and wine, and beer and spirits, there is another thing which is used by a great many people, but which is not really necessary to enable people to live, and that is tobacco, and tobacco, therefore, is taxed too. There are also a good many other things, such as lace, raisins, and scent, which are taxed in the same way; but the most important by far are those I have mentioned to you—namely, tea, wine, beer, spirits, and tobacco.

XXXII.
Who Pays Indirect Taxes?

1. But perhaps you will ask what I mean after all by saying that you or I ever pay part of these taxes, because it is quite true that I said just now that the money was paid to the Government by the merchants who brought the goods to England from foreign countries. Wait a minute, and you will see that I was right after all.

2. Suppose the merchant who brings the tea into the country had no tax to pay, he would have nothing to think about but how to make a profit by selling his tea to his customers. He would have to get back enough money to repay him for what he had spent in growing the tea in China or India, and in bringing it over in a ship to this country; and beyond this he would have to make a profit, that is to say, to get something over and above what he had spent to pay him for his trouble and to help him to grow richer.

3. But then remember that for every pound of tea which he brings over, he has to pay a tax of sixpence; and if he were not to reckon up the tax as part of what he had spent, he would soon find that instead of making a profit upon the sale of the tea he was really losing money. What must he do, therefore? It is plain that for every penny which he pays as a tax to the Government, he must add at least a penny to the price which he charges to his customers.

SOME INDIRECT TAX-PAYERS.

4. Now, who are really his customers? Why, of course, you and I, and every one of us who drinks tea, and it is you and I and all the other tea-drinkers who really pay the tax upon tea. And so it is quite true what I said—namely, that every time you drink a cup of tea you are paying an indirect tax.

The Fewer Taxes the Better

5. Of course, the fewer taxes people have to pay, the better, whether the taxes be direct, like those on carriages and dogs, or indirect, like those on tea and tobacco. For in either case, the money

which is paid really comes out of the pockets of the people of this country, and many of them find it hard enough, as you know, to make their living, and to pay for their rent, their living, and their clothes. Therefore, it is of the greatest importance that as few taxes as possible should be laid upon the country; and if they have to be paid, it is better that they should be paid in the way which causes least suffering and trouble to those who are very poor.

Taxes on Bread

6. Not many years ago, all the corn that came into England was taxed, and of course, those who bought the corn, or rather those who bought the bread which was made from this corn, were the payers of this tax. The consequence of this was that bread became very dear, and all the millions of people throughout the country had to pay a high price for their loaf.

RICHARD COBDEN.
From photograph by W. & D. Downey, 57 & 61, Ebury Street.

7. Now, bread is necessary for everybody, and the number of those who could not afford to pay for a dear loaf was very great. On every side, complaints were heard, and in many places, there was much suffering and distress because of the dearness of bread caused by the tax upon corn.

8. In many districts,

riots and disturbances broke out, and the people, threatened with hunger, and angry with an unjust and harmful law, committed acts of violence, which, however unwise they may have been in themselves, showed how real and how great was the suffering which had been caused.

9. For a long time, those who wished to see the corn tax done away with, and who thought it both unjust and unwise to tax the food of the people, were unsuccessful in their efforts; but at last, in the year 1846, an Act of Parliament called the "Act for the Repeal of the Corn Laws," was passed, and this tax upon the people's food was done away with for ever.

10. The men who took the leading part in bringing about this great change will always be famous in English history. They were—Richard Cobden, John Bright, Charles Villiers, and Sir Robert Peel. Now, I think I have told you enough to give you an idea of what taxes are, who it is pays them, and how they are collected.

Parliament Votes the Taxes

11. There is one more thing to be remembered about them, and it is this—that, nowadays, it is those who pay the taxes who decide what they are to be, and how they are to be collected. This was not always so. There was a time when the king was accustomed to make the people pay whatever sums he chose. It was not long, however, before the injustice of this plan was felt; and as far back as the reign of King Henry III, the Parliament of England claimed the right, which it has never since given up, of deciding how much the people of England should pay.

12. Of course, it is not the same thing to claim a right and to get others to recognize it. For many hundred years after the reign of Henry III, there were attempts made by the kings to levy taxes

SIR ROBERT PEEL.

without consulting Parliament, and very often Parliament was unable to prevent this being done.

13. One of the chief differences which brought about the Civil War in Charles I's time, and which ended in the King losing his head, and in Oliver Cromwell being made Protector, was a dispute as to the payment of a tax called Ship-money, which the king wished to collect illegally. He was resisted in his attempt by a very famous member of the House of Commons, John Hampden by name; and though at

JOHN BRIGHT.

first, Hampden seemed likely to suffer for his boldness, in the end, the cause for which he gave his life was victorious; and now, in our day, there is no longer any dispute as to the right of Parliament, and Parliament alone, to vote taxes.

CHAPTER XV.
OUR DUTY TOWARDS FOREIGN COUNTRIES – PART I

"Do unto others as you would they should do unto you."

XXXIII.
The "Barbarians"

1. THE ancient Greeks had a strange way of speaking of all foreigners, no matter who they were, as "Barbarians." It was the same whether they spoke of the educated and civilized people of Egypt, of the luxurious and warlike Persians, or of the wild Scythian tribes who passed their lives in a half-savage state in the country north of the Black Sea. To the Greek, they were alike one and all—Egyptian, Persian, Scythian; they were uncouth, outlandish, barbarian—in a word, not Greek.

2. In the same way, at the present time, the Chinese also speak of all foreigners—English, Americans, French, Germans—without any distinction, as "Barbarians." China, to the Chinese, is the only country in the world. If there be any other countries in the world, they are unimportant and uncivilized, and the people who live in them are only "Barbarians."

Look at Home

3. It is easy to laugh at the Greeks of old, and at the Chinese of the present day, and to wonder at any people being so foolish as to think that no one nation but their own deserves to be called civilized.

But after all, it is not quite certain that if we were to look carefully we might not find something of the same kind nearer home. England is so shut off from the rest of the world by being an island that very many English people never see foreign countries at all, and very seldom see the people who live in them. Some of us, perhaps, know a Frenchman, or a German, or an Italian, but we know very little indeed of the countries from which they come, and when we speak of them as foreigners we often talk as if they were something quite different from ourselves.

4. Sometimes you will hear people, both grown-up men and women, as well as children, talk scornfully of foreigners as if they thought them in some way inferior to themselves. And others you will hear talking as if all foreigners were their enemies, and as if it was the most natural thing in the world for Englishmen and Frenchmen, or Englishmen and Germans, to be always quarrelling, always hating each other, always trying to take advantage of each other.

5. Whenever you hear anybody talking in this way, or whenever you feel inclined yourselves to talk or to think in such a fashion, it will be time for you to remember the Greeks and the Chinese, and to ask yourselves whether it was quite fair to laugh at them for holding such foolish opinions about their neighbours.

The Result of Ignorance

6. After all, it is really just the same reason that made the Greeks of old, and the Chinese of to-day, talk of "Barbarians," that makes people in this country say harsh and unjust things about Germans, French, or Italians, and makes them hate or despise people of whom they really know nothing. The reason in both cases is ignorance.

7. A boy who lives till he is twenty in a little country town, and never goes out of it, will, perhaps, think that there is nothing in the world so high as the steeple of the parish church, and no river so broad as the brook which runs under it. But directly he leaves his

home and travels abroad, he begins to find out that there are a great many things in the world which he has not seen, and a good many, too, which he has never even heard of, and before very long he will stop talking about the wonders of his own home, unless he wants to be laughed at by the people whom he meets.

How Travel Teaches Us

8. And so, in the same way, it is easy enough for us, as long as we live in this country, to persuade ourselves that there is very little that is good, or well done, or well arranged outside it. But directly we cross the sea, we shall find out that there are, besides England, other great countries, each with its own beauties, and its own advantages; excelling us in some points, inferior to us in others.

9. In each country in turn, we shall find men, women, and children, living useful and happy lives, such as we are accustomed to at home, and though we shall notice at first a great many differences in the manners and customs of those whom we see, the more we know of the people and their ways, the less real difference shall we find between them and ourselves.

10. Wherever we go, we shall find men and women working hard and honestly for their daily bread, we shall find children going to school, young men and women falling in love and marrying, men and women of all ages doing good in a hundred different ways which are not the less useful because they are not quite the ways we are accustomed to.

11. The first time we see a foreigner, and hear him talk, we are sure to be struck by his strangeness and by the difficulty of understanding him; and the first time we set foot in a foreign country, we are sure to notice directly all the things which are unlike what we have been accustomed to at home. But if we get to know the foreigner better, or if we spend a longer time in the foreign country, we are nearly

certain to find out that neither the one nor the other is really half so strange as we first thought.

An Example

12. There is a story which teaches us a very good lesson about not laughing at things just because they seem strange, or despising other people because their manners and customs appear at first sight to be different from ours. As often as not, you will find out that the strange thing which you are laughing at is really to be found quite near home, only that we call it by a different name and use it in another fashion. I will tell you the story in the next chapter.

CHAPTER XVI.

OUR DUTY TOWARDS FOREIGN COUNTRIES – PART II

"There are folk beyond the mountains."—*German Proverb*.

XXXIV.
A Strange Country

1. ONCE upon a time, a certain man was asked to give an account of his travels. "I will tell you," said he, "what I saw in a remarkable country which I lately visited, and in which I found a curious people whose manners and customs were as strange as they were ridiculous."

2. "The country in question was an island, and I believe I am not the only person who has visited it, and those others who have succeeded in reaching its shores will, I am certain, confirm the truth of my story, and convince you that what I say of this particular tribe is no collection of travellers' tales, but a true account of a real people who are not without some understanding, and certain traces of civilisation."

An Account of the Tribe[15]

3. "I was once, about this time of the year, in a country where it was very cold, and the poor inhabitants had much ado to keep themselves from starving. They were clad partly in the skins of

15 The greater portion of this chapter is taken from Mrs. Barbauld's charming work *Evenings at Home.*

144

beasts made soft and smooth by a particular art, but chiefly in garments made from the outer covering of a middle-sized quadruped which they were so cruel as to strip off his back while he was alive."

4. "They dwelt in habitations, part of which was sunk underground. The materials were either stones or earth hardened by fire; and so violent in that country were the storms of wind and rain, that many of them covered their roofs all over with stones. The walls of their houses had holes to let in the light; but to prevent the cold air and wet from coming in, they were covered with a sort of transparent stone, made artificially of melted sand or flints."

Their Diet

5. "Their diet too was remarkable. Some of them ate fish that had been hung up in the smoke till they were quite dry and hard; and along with it, they ate either the roots of plants, or a sort of coarse black cake made of powdered seeds. These were the poorer class; the richer had a whiter kind of cake, which they were fond of daubing over with a greasy matter that was the product of a large animal among them. This grease they used, too, in almost all their dishes, and when fresh, it really was not unpalatable."

6. "They likewise devoured the flesh of many birds and beasts when they could get it; and ate the leaves and other parts of a variety of vegetables growing in the country, some absolutely raw, others variously prepared by the aid of fire. Another great article of food was the curd of milk, pulped into a hard mass and salted."

"FOR DRINK, THEY MADE GREAT USE OF THE WATER IN WHICH CERTAIN DRY LEAVES HAD BEEN STEEPED."

Their Drink

7. "For drink, they made great use of the water in which certain dry leaves had been steeped. These leaves, I was told, came from a great distance. They had likewise a method of preparing a liquor of the seeds of a grass-like plant steeped in water, with the addition of a bitter herb, and then set to work or ferment. I was prevailed upon to taste it, and thought it at first nauseous enough, but in time I

liked it pretty well. When a large quantity of the ingredients is used, it becomes perfectly intoxicating."

8. "But what astonished me most was their use of a liquor so excessively hot and pungent that it seemed like liquid fire. I once got a mouthful of it by mistake, taking it for water, which it resembles in appearance; but I thought it would instantly have taken away my breath. Indeed, people are not unfrequently killed by it; and yet many of them will swallow it greedily whenever they can get it. This, too, is said to be prepared from the seeds above mentioned, which are innocent and even salutary in their natural state, though made to yield such a pernicious juice."

Their Strange Birds and Plants

9. "I was glad enough to leave this cold climate; and about half a year after, I fell in with a people enjoying a delicious temperature of air, and a country full of beauty and verdure. The trees and shrubs were furnished with a great variety of fruits, which, with other vegetable products, constituted a large part of the food of the inhabitants. I particularly relished certain berries growing in bunches, some white and some red, of a very pleasant sourish taste, and so transparent that we might see the seeds at their very centre."

10. "Here were whole fields full of extremely odoriferous flowers, which, they told me, were succeeded by pods bearing seeds, that afforded good nourishment to man and beast. A great variety of birds enlivened the groves and woods; among which I was entertained with one, that without any teaching spoke almost as plainly as a parrot, though indeed it was all the repetition of a single word."

Their Manners

11. "The people were tolerably gentle and civilised, and possessed many of the arts of life. Their dress was very various. Many were clad only in a thin cloth made of the long fibres of the stalk of

a plant cultivated for the purpose, which they prepared by soaking in water, and then beating with large mallets."

Their Clothes

12. "Others wore cloth woven from a sort of vegetable wool growing in pods upon bushes. But the most singular material was a fine glossy stuff, used chiefly by the richer classes, which, as I was credibly informed, is manufactured out of the webs of caterpillars—a most wonderful circumstance if we consider the immense number of caterpillars necessary to the production of so large a quantity of the stuff as I saw used."

13. "This people are very fantastic in their dress, especially the women, whose apparel consists of a great number of articles impossible to be described, and strangely disguising the natural form of the body. In some instances, they seem to be very cleanly, but in others, the Hottentots can scarce go beyond them, particularly in the management of their hair, which is all stiffened with the fat of swine and other animals, mixed up with powders of various colours and ingredients."

Their Odd Habits

14. "Like most Indian nations, they use feathers in the head-dress. One thing surprised me much, which was, that they bring up in their houses an animal of the tiger kind, with formidable teeth and claws, which, notwithstanding its natural ferocity, is played with and caressed by the most timid and delicate of their women. The language of this nation seems very harsh and unintelligible to a foreigner, yet they converse among one another with great ease and quickness."

What is the name of the Country?

15. You do not want me to go any further with this story. You have found me out already, I am sure; and you know that the strange

country about which the traveller told his tale was nothing but our own "England," and that all the odd things that he described were only what you and I are accustomed to every day of our lives.

16. You know that the grease used in the dishes of the islanders is neither more nor less than butter, and that the large animal which produces it is the cow. The dried leaves which are soaked in water are tea-leaves; and if you use your wits you will easily find out that all the other things that are mentioned are, after all, old friends with new faces, and only seem odd because they are described in a way you are not accustomed to.

CHAPTER XVII

OUR DUTY TOWARDS FOREIGN COUNTRIES – PART III

"Hatred is the child of ignorance and the father of strife."

XXXV.
A Lesson

1. WHAT I want you to learn from the story in the last chapter is not to judge foreigners and the countries from which they come too hastily. I want you to learn that it is foolish as well as wicked to say that all the people in another country are bad, or stupid, or ridiculous, because they think or do something of which you do not approve. It is foolish, because it generally happens that if we were a little wiser, we should see that those whom we laugh at have a very good reason for doing what they do.

Be sure of your Facts

2. If you were to see a man go and lay the foundations of his house within two or three yards of the sea at Ramsgate or Morecambe, you would laugh at him, and tell him that when the tide rose, he and his proposed house would soon be many feet under water. And probably, if you were to see a man do the same thing at Naples in Italy, or at Trieste in Austria, you would laugh with just as much good-will as you would at home.

3. But though you might laugh with as much goodwill, you would certainly not do it with half so much reason, for though there is a tide

in the North Sea and a tide in the Irish Channel, there is no tide in the Mediterranean Sea, and just because you did not know this one fact, which everybody who lives on the shores of the Mediterranean knows quite well, you would have fallen into a foolish mistake, and the laugh would have been against you, instead of on your side.

4. And so you see, until you know as much about other people's affairs as they do themselves, it is not very safe to laugh at them or to find fault with them.

5. And, as I told you, it is not only foolish, but wicked, to judge too hastily about the actions of foreign peoples about whom we know very little; for that is how quarrels between nations spring up, and such quarrels, as you know, often end in war, the most terrible misfortune which can overtake a country.

6. You will be astonished when you read history to find how small are the matters about which great quarrels have arisen and great wars been fought.

The Story of the Two Knights.

7. I daresay you know the story of the knights and the shield: how, in the olden time, two knights riding to meet each other from different directions saw hanging over their path a shield. "What a beautiful golden shield," said the one. "Golden!" replied the other; "silver, you mean." "The shield is golden, and it is golden that I mean," said the first knight. "You must surely be a little weak of sight," says number two, "not to be able to tell gold from silver."

8. And so, the story runs, a pretty quarrel began, and only ended by the knights settling their difference in the knightly fashion of their day, and having a battle there and then to prove that their respective opinions were right; though how they could prove much by running each other through the body is not very plain.

9. At last, as they both lay bleeding and exhausted upon the plain, there came by a friar. To him, as he staunched their wounds,

THE KNIGHTS AND THE SHIELD.

they explained the ground of their quarrel, and asked him as a fair-minded person to decide which of them was really in the right, for inasmuch as neither of them had won the battle, neither could say that his view was the correct one.

10. "Tell us, holy father," they said, "is the shield gold or silver?"

"Poor deluded men," replied the friar; "is this the cause of your quarrel? How easily you could have solved it with a little patience. Neither of you is right, neither of you wrong. Look at this shield; one side is gold, and the other silver. If you had only tried to look at the question from both sides you would not be lying in this sorry plight."

The Moral.

11. The moral of this story is plain enough. The two knights fought not in order to find out whether the shield was gold or silver, for it did not matter the least to either of them what it was made of, but they fought to satisfy their own pride, and because both of them thought it was finer to fight about a difference of opinion than to find out in a reasonable way what the real truth was, and whether, when they knew the truth, it mattered the least bit in the world to either of them on which side it lay.

XXXVI.
How Wars Are Begun.

1. It is wonderful how often the great countries of the world have followed the example of the two knights, and have quarrelled about the very smallest matters, and have entered upon great and terrible wars simply because their pride was wounded, and because they would not try to look at both sides of a question. When we consider how horrible a thing war is, and how great is the suffering which it inflicts not only upon those who fight, but upon all those to whom it brings sorrow, poverty, and pain at home, it becomes plain that anyone who helps to bring about a war is a very bad citizen and a very false friend of his country.

2. And yet there are always to be found men who are ready when any little difference arises between two countries to try and make their countrymen follow the example of the two knights. They will only look at their side of the shield, and will never stop to think that

somebody with eyes as good as theirs sees something quite different on the other side.

3. And when they have once started the foolish quarrel, they do all they can, by saying bitter and unjust things of their opponents, to make it impossible for either side to look at the matter coolly—to take down the shield, and turn it over, and settle in a reasonable way whether there be anything worth fighting about at all.

Enemies of Their Country.

4. Such men as these are enemies of their country, and we should all take the greatest pains not to be found among their number.

5. The safest way to do this, and the best way to do good service to the country, is for everyone, man or woman, boy or girl, to be even more careful in what they say about foreigners and foreign countries than about what they say of their own countrymen and their own country.

Some Good Rules to Remember.

6. Always be civil and courteous to a foreigner; in the first place, because it is your duty to be civil and courteous to everybody, and especially to those who are strangers and far from their own friends.

7. In the second place, because as you behave to them, so will they judge of you, and when they return to their own country they will help to win friends or enemies for England accordingly as they have found those Englishmen and Englishwomen whom they have met friendly or not.

8. And lastly, be civil and courteous to foreigners, because the danger of being uncivil and discourteous is so great, and is a danger not only to you but to all your fellow-countrymen.

9. Always stand up for the honour of your own country, but remember that others are equally bound to stand up for the honour of theirs, and that the honour of your own country can never be

advanced by the people who live in it fighting for what is unjust and wrong. Turn back to Chapter IX. and read the words at the beginning of it. In them, you will find what Edmund Burke, one of the wisest of our statesmen, thought about war and about the objects for which alone it could rightly be begun.

10. These are his words: - "The blood of man should never be shed but to redeem the blood of man. It is well shed for our family, for our friends, for our God, for our country, for our kind. The rest is vanity; the rest is crime."

CHAPTER XVIII.

EDUCATION.

"The fear of the Lord is the beginning of wisdom."
"Knowledge is power."

XXXVII.
What Education Means.

1. IN the earlier chapters of this book, you have been learning something about the laws and how they are made, something about the way in which our country is governed, something about the reasons why people have to pay rates and taxes. It is right and useful that every English boy and girl should be taught to understand something of the government of their own country, but perhaps some of you think that whether you know much or little about these other matters, at least you all know about education, what it means, and what is the use of it.

2. When you hear people talking of education, it makes you think at once about going to school. Well, education means something more than going to school, but still, going to school is one great part of education, and it is just the part that we are going to think about now. If I were to begin by asking you why you come to school, I expect you would answer quite rightly, that you come in order to learn.

3. And then if I were to go on to ask you what it is you come to learn, you would most likely answer, reading, writing, and arithmetic. That is quite true too, and yet there is something besides, which is

156

quite as important—indeed more important—than even reading and writing.

Some School-room Lessons.

4. In many schools, there is a board hanging up which tells of some of the great lessons that have to be taught and learned in school. And the lessons that this board speaks about are not geography, or arithmetic, or dictation, but "habits of punctuality, of good manners and language, of cleanliness and neatness." The board says that care must be taken to teach the scholars these les-

IN SCHOOL.

sons, and to make them feel the importance of "cheerful obedience to duty, of consideration and respect for others, and of honour and truthfulness in word and act."

5. These words on this board were written by the gentlemen at the great house in London called the Education Office, who look after all the national schools and board schools throughout the country. Very likely you have just those words hanging up in your own school, very likely you have often read them, but have you ever thought about them?

Precept and Practice.

6. It is quite certain that if anyone thoroughly masters these lessons while he is at school, he will become, if he lives to grow up, a good and a useful citizen; but if he has not learned these lessons, then though he may get a great deal of learning of a different kind, it will do him more harm than good. If a boy goes on all through his school life cheating at lessons whenever he had the opportunity, you would know that he had not learned "truthfulness in act," and you would have very little hope of his growing up an honourable, fair-dealing man.

7. And, again, if a boy takes advantage of his strength to tease and oppress those who are weaker than himself, you are sure that he has not learned "consideration and respect for others," and that he is likely to become one of those miserable people who care for nothing greater or higher than their own selfish pleasure.

8. So, once more, if a boy does his work sulkily and unwillingly, doing it only because he is obliged, and trying all he can to shirk it, then you know he has not learned the lesson of "cheerful obedience to duty," and you feel that such a boy will never be a useful citizen or do good service to his country, for he "shrinks when hard service must be done; he even grudges taking enough trouble to do his common everyday work well."

9. So you will see for yourselves the truth of what I have said about the importance of these lessons beyond all other lessons. Over and over again, England has been faithfully and gloriously served by men who never had the chance of learning to read or write; but never in her whole history has she been truly served by men who had not learned these other lessons of honour and truthfulness, of care for others, of obedience to duty.

The King who could not Write.

10. You most of you know that in old days education was much less widely spread than it is now. You still find plenty of old people, and some middle-aged people too, who cannot read a book or sign their own names; if we could go back a hundred years we should find the number of them still greater, and if we go back 800 years we shall find a king of England in the same position, unable to sign his own name.

11. In the Cathedral library at Canterbury, I have seen a piece of old yellow parchment with the name of William the Conqueror written upon it. After the name comes a mark, such as some uneducated people nowadays make when they are unable to write their own names. So on this old parchment, some learned man had written the king's name for him, and the king had put his mark against it, to show that it was all right. Is it not strange to think that the William the Conqueror about whom you read in your histories did not know how to sign his own name?

XXXVIII.
Schools and School Boards.

1. Sometimes old people will tell you that the reason why they never learned to read or write was that there was no school near where they lived. Until lately, there were not nearly enough schools

in England, and even now there are not as many as are needed, but new ones are being built every year, and there are a great many more now than there used to be.

2. The Government has said that in every town and village there must be enough schools for all the children in the place to go to, and if the schools that are built already are not big enough, a certain number of people are elected to form what is called the "School Board." It is the duty of the school board to see that proper schools are provided, and that the children who are not going to the old schools go to the new ones.

3. The expense of building these schools is paid out of the public money, because they are meant for the public good. It is better for the whole neighbourhood that the children should be taught than that they should grow up in ignorance, and so it is fair that every ratepayer in the neighbourhood should take his share in paying for the school.

4. And now we will suppose a place where there are plenty of schools, either church schools, or board schools, or half-time schools.

Scholars.

5. The schools are there, but you will agree with me that if they are to stand empty, they might as well never have been built. Clearly, we must have the scholars to fill them.

6. The best thing of all is when the children come of themselves, regularly and punctually, but if the children are careless themselves about coming, and the parents do not take pains about sending them, then the school-board officer or attendance officer has to go to the house and find out why the child does not come to school. There may be some satisfactory reason, and then the child is excused; but if there is no good reason, the parent is first warned, and then, if he does not pay any attention to the warning, fined.

7. This compelling children to go to school is called "compulsion," or "compulsory education."

8. Sometimes it seems hard that children should be compelled to attend school when their parents would be very glad of their help at home, but then we have to remember that it is really better in the end—better for the parents, better for the children, and better for the whole country—that the children should be regularly taught while they are young than that they should have the great disadvantage of growing up in ignorance.

School Attendance.

9. It is a great mistake to think that if you come to school irregularly, no one suffers but yourself. You suffer most, it is true, but the whole school suffers too. You see it when the examination day comes round, when the inspector comes, and refuses to pass many of the scholars.

10. It is very disappointing for the master to have to say, "I have a hundred scholars on the books, but some of them have attended so irregularly I cannot present them for examination;" or suppose, on the other hand, that they are examined and that they fail; either way, they bring discredit upon the school. You would think it very hard if you had to suffer for someone's wrong-doing, and yet, is it not just as hard if the school gets a less good report because you and others like you have been idle?

The Credit of the School.

11. Always remember that the well-doing of a school depends on the well-doing of every scholar in it. The school board may build schools, the law may oblige children to attend, the master may give all his time and thought to teaching his classes, but neither school board, nor law, nor master, can force a child to do his best if he does not care about it himself. And yet it is upon the children, as

well as the teachers, setting themselves to do their very best, that the success and honour of the school depend.

12. It is true that the law has forbidden any child under thirteen years of age to go to work until he has passed certain standards, but as soon as he has completed his fourteenth year, he can leave school whether he has passed them or not. Some lazy scholars seem to think that when once they have passed their standards and got their labour certificates, they have done all that is required, and that it makes no difference whether they learn any more or not—but what a mistake they are making!

XXXIX.
Reading, Writing, and Something More.

1. Reading and writing are so common now, that just to be able to read and write and cipher will not enable anyone to get on in life. A boy must not only have learnt to read, he must have attended to what he has read and got good from it; he must not only know how to do a sum when it is set before him, but he must be able to apply his school arithmetic rules to the business of daily life, and know how to calculate measurements.

2. Some of you may have heard the story of Opie, the painter, when someone asked him what he mixed his colours with. "Brains, sir," answered the painter, meaning that instead of going by any fixed rules out of a book, he thought for himself exactly what would be best for the piece of work he had in hand.

Eyes and no Eyes.

3. Take the case of two boys. They may know just the same amount to start with; they may be in the same standard, but if one of the two tries to make use out of school of the knowledge that he has gained in class, and to add more to it, he will soon leave far

behind the other, who, as soon as the book is shut, thinks no more of what he has been reading.

4. Book-learning is a great help, but it can never stand in the place of observation and thought.

5. Take, for example, a lesson in Physical Geography. All the boys may have learnt from the same book; they may all of them remember a good deal of what they have read, and be able to repeat it almost in the words of the book, but most likely they have never thought of noticing for themselves any of the things which they have been reading about.

6. But suppose there is one boy who, when he is out walking, remembers what he has been reading, and compares it with what he sees round about him; such a boy will find, as soon as he begins to use his own eyes, that there are a whole number of questions that he wants to have answered, and that perhaps his book may help to answer for him; he will find that he has learnt enough in his walk to make the next geography lesson doubly interesting.

How to Rise.

7. At a great many schools, more especially in towns, there are now what are called *exhibitions*, or scholarships—that is to say, money prizes given to help a boy forward in his education. A boy who passes all his standards, and does well at school, may win one of these prizes, which will enable him to go on to a higher kind of school, where Latin and Greek and many other subjects are taught. If he does well here too, he may get another scholarship which will enable him, when he is old enough, to pass on to one of the Universities, it may be to Oxford or Cambridge; and in time he may become a doctor, a lawyer, or a clergyman, and rise to the head of his profession.

Compulsion.

8. As I told you, education is now *compulsory*—that is to say, every parent is compelled to have his child educated. This was not always so. It was only in the year 1870 that Mr. Forster brought in a Bill in Parliament, which afterwards became the Education Act. By this Act, it was made part of the law that in every part of the country where the majority of the people wished it, all the children in the district might be compelled to go to school; and since that time, it has become the law all over England that every child should have some education, and so be able to have a chance of rising and gaining a living when it grows up.

9. For you must understand that nowadays, when all the children in foreign countries are taught in good schools, it is quite necessary that English children should not be behindhand; otherwise, all the work would certainly go to those who knew best how to do it, and the trade of our country would go to foreigners. It is not in England

UNIVERSITY COLLEGE.   THE UNIVERSITY CHURCH.   QUEEN'S COLLEGE.
HIGH STREET, OXFORD.

only that children are compelled to go to school; but they are equally obliged to do so in America, in Germany, and in France.

Three Reasons for Going to School.

10. I have now given you the reasons why you should be glad to go to school, and to learn all you can while you are there.

11. In the first place, because the more you learn, the more you will enjoy all the great books that have been written, the better you will understand the wonderful works of Nature, and the better use you will be able to make of its treasures.

12. In the second place, you should be glad to go to school, because by training your mind, and learning what history, geography, and science can teach, you will be better able to serve your country and to be a good citizen.

13. And, lastly, you should be glad to go to school, because it is only by the instruction you get there that you can hope to get on in your trade or profession, whatever it may be, and to prevent being left behind by cleverer workers and quicker hands in foreign countries.

CHAPTER XIX.

THRIFT.

"A penny saved is a penny gained."

XL.
Every One Ought to Save.

1. EVERYBODY in the country ought to try and save money against a rainy day, so that in old age, in time of sickness or distress, he may have something to fall back upon, and not be dependent upon others for support.

Why?

2. I need not spend much time in telling you why this is so, and why it is the duty of every man and woman, and, indeed, of every child, to put aside money in the savings bank, or in some other place where it will be kept safe and be ready for use in time of need. You have only got to think a little for yourselves, and you will see the reason as plainly as I can tell it to you.

3. In the first place, it is a duty which every man owes to himself. Those who are young, and healthy, and strong, find it sometimes hard to understand how terrible a thing it is to have bad times without any money saved.

4. Over and over again it happens that a good workman is unwise enough to depend upon his skill and his strength, and neglects to look forward. As long as there is work for him to do, or as long as his health and strength remain, he receives his wages

166

and lives comfortably. But one day work becomes slack, or he falls ill, or an accident happens to him, and then suddenly and without any warning he finds himself face to face with poverty; unable to provide his food, unable to pay his rent, unable to pay his doctor.

Save Against Old Age.

5. Again, it may happen that a man has been fortunate enough to pass through the greater part of his life without any such misfortunes as those I have spoken of, and at last he finds old age coming on. Then, if he has saved nothing, he has to look forward to ending his days in sorrow and in misery, in a home without comfort or convenience, or it may be in the workhouse itself.

6. In order that a man may not live in distress and die in poverty, it is his duty to save money.

Save to Help Others.

7. But there are few men and few women who have no one but themselves to think of. Husbands must provide for their wives, wives must help their husbands, parents must bring up and take care of their children. And so, if illness or accident overtake any member of a family, there is generally sure to be some other member of the family who will have to bear the loss as well as the actual sufferer, and who will be unable to bear it without loss and trouble, unless a little money has been saved.

8. A man may be a good workman, and may never be idle or sick, yet if his wife or child be ill, he will have to spend money to relieve them just the same as he would have to do were he himself ill.

9. In order, therefore, that a man may support his family in time of trouble, it is his duty to save money.

Save to Keep Out of the Workhouse.

10. And lastly, supposing a man or woman does not save, but when hard times come, or misfortune occurs, or old age is at hand, is unable to earn anything to support life, and is thus forced to go to the workhouse or to accept relief from others, then we shall see directly that a real injustice is being done. For, of course, the workhouse is not kept up for nothing, and the relief that is given by the parish is paid for by somebody; and that somebody is really the people who pay the rates.

11. It very often happens that those who pay rates have hard enough work to get their own living, and it is hard that they who have managed to save and to keep out of the workhouse should have to pay for the support of those who have been more careless, and who, by their carelessness, have found their way into the workhouse.

12. In order, therefore, that a man should not become a burden upon his neighbours, it is his duty to save money.

One More Reason for Saving.

13. These are three very good reasons why people should save and put by money for a rainy day, and there is one other reason which I must not miss out in a book which tells about our duties as "Good Citizens." Not only are saving and thrift most important and necessary for particular men and women, but it is of the greatest use to the country generally that all its citizens should be thrifty and saving.

14. It is only those who are free from want and poverty who can be contented, and it is only a country in which the greater number of the inhabitants are contented that can be really strong.

15. For all these reasons, therefore, it is a good thing to be thrifty and to save.

XLI.
How to Save.

1. But how are we to set about saving—what is the best way to do it? There was a time when people used to think there was no better way of saving than putting their money into an old stocking and hiding it away. I dare say there are some old folks who do this still. But it is not a very wise plan to follow nowadays.

2. Supposing a man earns a shilling or a pound when he is thirty years old, and puts it away in a safe place till he is fifty. When he goes to look for it, he will find just exactly what he first saved, whether it be a shilling, or a pound, or twenty pounds, and no more. All the twenty years that the money has been laid up it will have been useless.

Savings Banks.

3. But supposing the same man, instead of locking his money up, goes and puts it in the bank, then, at the end of twenty years, instead of finding just what he first put in, he will find more than half as much again added to what he first earned. For the bank, instead of letting the money lie idle, will use it, lending it to people who are in want of it, spending it upon work which brings a profit, and so on, and they will pay the man who left the money with them so much a year for the use of it.

4. This payment is called interest, and by adding the interest together, year after year, a man's savings will soon be doubled.

The Post Office Bank.

5. It is not necessary to have a great deal of money to be able to put it into a bank. All over the country, there are post office savings banks, where anybody can put in any sum from a shilling up to thirty pounds, and be sure of getting interest paid to him in return. Every boy and girl, therefore, can begin to put money into the bank. All

that is necessary is to go to the post office, get a savings bank book, and pay in the money which is to be saved.

Take Care of the Pence.

6. There is even an easier way of saving little sums than this; for now you can get at the post office little cards divided into twelve squares, which are on purpose to help people to save[16]. Each square is meant to contain a penny stamp, which you can buy and stick on. When there are twelve stamps on the card, all you have got to do is to take it to the post office again, and in exchange for the twelve penny stamps, one shilling will be added to your savings and put down in your bank book. So you see there is no reason why every penny should not be saved and put in the bank.

What Pennies Can Do.

7. It is wonderful how much can be done by saving little sums regularly. One of the most useful ways of saving is to put by money when one is young to buy what is called a pension—that is to say, a regular weekly payment to be received when one grows old, or becomes sick. For instance, if a young man at the age of nineteen puts by eightpence a week, or only a little more than a penny a day, he can be sure when he reaches sixty years of age to receive a pension of 5s. a week, and thus, whatever happens, he will never be quite without support in his old age.

8. Of course, it might happen that he died before reaching sixty years of age, and it would be hard in such a case if all the money he had put by were lost. Fortunately, it is not lost, for in case of a man's death, whatever he may have paid is given to his relations.

9. In the same way, by saving little sums when you are young,

16   At the end of this book you will find one of these post-office cards, on which you may begin at once to put stamps. When it is full you can tear it out, take it to the post office, and thus put a shilling in the bank.

you can insure your lives; that is to say, you can be sure that on your death a round sum of money will be paid to your family. In this way, a man who has insured his life can be certain that when he dies his wife and children will not be left to starve.

10. It is a terrible thing for a man to feel that the comfort and welfare of those who are dearest to him depend upon his life only, and that in case of his death they have only misery and poverty to look forward to.

Clubs and Friendly Societies.

11. Besides all the ways of saving money in which the Government helps, there are the ways which are provided by what are called friendly societies or benefit clubs.

12. Those who join these clubs agree to pay so much a year to the club, and in return, they are sure of receiving help when they fall sick, or become too old to work. Each society or club has a different name, and some of them, such as the Foresters and Oddfellows, have a very large number of members and a great many subscriptions. They are very good institutions, not only because they are the means of helping those who are sick or unable to work, but because they encourage people to be thrifty and to save.

Provident Dispensaries.

13. Unfortunately, it is not so easy for women to save as for men, because in some of the friendly societies there are no arrangements made for helping women when they are sick and out of work. Women have often so much pain and sickness to bear that it is a great pity there are not better means of helping them.

14. However, in many places there are what are called Provident Dispensaries, that is to say, places where medicine and a doctor's help can be got by all those who have made a regular weekly or monthly payment. Women can always subscribe to these dispensaries, and

they should certainly do so, for thus they can guard against being left without medicine and without anything to soothe their pain when they are in suffering and sickness.

When to Begin Saving.

15. It is never too early to begin to save. Remember this while you are young, and if you are wise, you will begin at once to put by money in the bank, for a penny saved is not only a penny gained, it becomes before long a penny-half-penny gained, and, if you wait long enough, twopence gained. Money that is wisely laid up is never idle, not only is it increasing from day to day and year to year, but every day it is helping to relieve the mind of the person who has saved it from anxiety and from the fear of being left in want and distress.

CHAPTER XX.

FREEDOM.

"It is the land that freemen till,
That sober-minded Freedom chose,
The land, where girt with friends or foes,
A man may speak the thing he will."—*Tennyson.*

XLII.
England is a Free Country.

1. I DARE SAY you have often heard people talk about England being a Free Country, and about the *Liberty* which we who live in England enjoy.

2. Fortunately for us, we live at a time when the very idea of being anything but free seems quite strange, and when some explanation is wanted of what is really meant by being without freedom and liberty.

3. But this was not always so. In times past, our ancestors were in many ways deprived of their freedom, and they enjoyed very little of the liberty which we now possess.

What Freedom Is.

4. But before I go any further and tell you how we at the present day have come to possess the freedom which our forefathers were without, I must try and explain to you what is meant by freedom, and why it is that we who enjoy it have so much to be thankful for.

5. Of course, when we use the word freedom, it is natural to think of somebody who has been actually imprisoned escaping

in some way from the place in which he is shut up, and there was indeed a time in this country when innocent men and women were not sure even of freedom from imprisonment without trial. I shall tell you something about that later on. But meanwhile, I want you to remember that there are other kinds of freedom which are even more important than that of merely going where one pleases.

6. Every one in this country is now free to think what he likes, to follow what religion he likes, to worship God in the way he chooses, and, moreover, he is free to try and persuade others of the truth of what he himself believes. Besides this, as you know, we have in this country what is called the *liberty of the press*, which means that a man may write and print what he wishes without interference.

7. Then again, we have freedom in buying and selling; we may buy what we like, and sell what we like. As I told you in another chapter, we have *freedom of election*: we may vote, without being interfered with, for the man whom we prefer to be a member for Parliament. Indeed, to put the whole matter quite shortly, we are free to do anything which is *not contrary to law, and which does not tend to injure our neighbours.*

What We Are Not Free to Do.

8. That is the only freedom which Englishmen are not allowed, and a moment's thought will show you that, if we were once allowed to do things which injured our neighbours, we should soon be in danger of losing our freedom ourselves. For instance, any of you, when you grow up and have votes, will be free, as I told you, to vote for any man you choose to be a member of Parliament, but you will not be free to try and compel other people to do so. For then you would at once be interfering with their freedom.

Trade Societies.

9. And so again, it is often very useful that those who are employed in the same kind of work—in weaving, in coal-mining, in building, in machine-making, or in any other trade—should join together, and make rules among themselves for their own advantage. When those engaged in one trade join together in this way, they form what is called a Trades Union, or Trade Society, and they are able to do much good, and the members are able to help one another in many ways.

10. Sometimes those who belong to a Trades Union make it a rule that none of them will take less than a certain wage for their work, and they all agree that unless they get as much as they think just and fair, they will not undertake the work at all. This is often a great help to the workers, and is sometimes the means of enabling them to get better wages and fairer treatment than they would if each man were to act for himself.

11. Sometimes, however, men belonging to societies of this kind have forgotten the true meaning of the word "freedom," and have tried to force others to obey their rules, even though they have never consented to do so, and do not wish to be bound by them. Directly they do this, they are no longer the friends of freedom, but the friends of tyranny, for though every man has a right to arrange what he will do about his own work, he has no right whatever to compel others to do the same.

12. It was when the Trades Unions were first started in this country that these mistakes were sometimes made, and great harm was done in some places by those who used violence against their fellow-workmen. But nowadays, fortunately, the true meaning of "freedom of labour" is better understood than it used to be, and all the great Trades Unions now condemn any interference with the freedom of others.

XLIII.
Unpleasant Trades.

1. Let me give you another instance of what I meant when I said that we were free to do anything which did not interfere with the freedom of others, or break the law.

2. There are a great many trades, such as the boiling of bones to make gelatine, the manufacture of vitriol, the tanning of hides for leather, and so on, which are very useful and very necessary, but which happen, for some reason or another, to be very unpleasant or very unwholesome; sometimes, as in the case of the tanning and bone-boiling, because of the smells which arise during the work; sometimes, as in the case of the making of vitriol, because of the poisonous fumes which escape.

3. Now, everybody is free to become a bone-boiler, or a tanner, or a manufacturer of vitriol, and as long as he carries on any of these trades without injuring or interfering with others, none will object. But it may sometimes happen that by opening his works in a particular neighbourhood he may do great damage to those who live around, and in that case the law will step in and say that either he must do the work elsewhere, or that he must do it in such a way that those who live near shall not be injured. For though we are free to carry on what trade we like, we are not free to carry it on to the injury of others.

Sale of Dangerous Things.

4. And so, once more, you remember I told you that in this country everyone was free to buy and sell what he chose. But here again, the same rule comes in. We are free to buy what we like and sell what we like, as long as we do not do any injury to others. But supposing a man sells gunpowder or poison, he is very likely to do great harm to his neighbours, for unless care is taken about the sale of such dangerous things, the gunpowder and the poison may eas-

ily fall into the hands of people who do not know their use, or who wish to use them for a bad purpose.

5. And so the law says that though the sale of cloth, and sugar, and boots, and hats, and so on, is free, yet the sale of gunpowder and poison is not to be free, and that only those persons shall be allowed to sell these things who have been specially allowed to do so.

Liberty of the Press.

6. In the same way, there are exceptions to the rule in other matters. I told you that we had in this country liberty of the press, that is to say, that everyone was free to write and to print what he chose. Nevertheless, there are some things which, although we enjoy this liberty, we are not allowed to write or to print. The same rule applies here as in the case of the sale of gunpowder and the manufacture of vitriol. We are free to do what we like, as long as by so doing we do not harm other people. But directly we begin to use our liberty to injure or annoy others, then the law will interfere and prevent us.

7. For instance, if a man were to write and print in a book or newspaper an accusation against one of his neighbours, saying that he was dishonest or untrustworthy in his trade, or had been guilty of some crime against the law, then his neighbour would have the right to go to law against him, and to have the writer punished either by being sent to prison or by being fined a sum of money.

The Abuse of Liberty.

8. A rule of this kind is indeed most useful, for in these days when newspapers and printing and the penny post have made it so easy for people to spread abroad reports about others, a terrible power is put into the hands of those who choose to use it for a bad purpose. It often happens that more harm is done to a man or a woman by spreading a false report, or telling an unkind story about

them, than could be inflicted upon them by any mere violence or actual bodily injury.

9. For instance, suppose anybody were to write a letter to the papers to say that a tradesman used false weights, or gave his customers sugar with sand in it, or tea which was half sweepings, there can be no doubt whatever that the poor grocer or tea-dealer, or whoever it might be, would suffer very much, and lose a great deal of custom. It would be no excuse for the person who made the charge to say afterwards that he found it was not true, for the harm would have been done, and the right and fair answer to make to him would be, "You should have taken the trouble to find out the truth before you accused your neighbour; you chose to judge him hastily and you must take the consequences."

The Power of Newspapers.

10. Unhappily, what is written in the newspapers nowadays is read by so many people and in so many different places, that when a false or unjust statement is once made, it is often quite impossible to undo the harm which it has occasioned, for many people read the charge who never see the reply to it. This ought to make people very careful indeed how they speak, and still more how they write harsh and cruel things about others. It is well indeed that the law of England, while it allows perfect liberty of the press to all who know how to use that liberty wisely, makes an exception in the case of those who use their liberty to injure others.

The Rule of Liberty.

11. These examples which I have been giving you are all intended to teach you what is the true meaning of freedom and liberty, and what is the right use to be made of it. You and I enjoy far greater liberty than our forefathers did, and very thankful we ought to be that we have no longer to suffer as they had for the right to think,

to write, to speak, to act as we please. But at the same time, we must remember that if more has been given to us, more will be expected of us.

12. We must never forget that we live in a world in which there are many millions of people besides ourselves, and that it is our bounden duty to live our own lives and to do our own work in such a way as not to interfere with or cause pain to others. The simple rule, "Do unto others as you would they should do unto you," is a very good one to bear in mind whenever we talk of our right to do this, that, and the other. We ought always to think of our duties together with our rights, and what our duties are, the rule you have just read will always tell you plainly enough.

13. You know that very young children and mad people are not allowed their freedom for fear they should do some harm to themselves or to others. It is only those who are supposed to have knowledge and experience to whom perfect liberty is allowed. By using our freedom wrongly we may show that like young children and madmen we are unfit to be trusted with it. It is by using it rightly, for the good of others as well as for our own good, that we can best show that we are wise enough and strong enough to possess so great a treasure as freedom really is.

CHAPTER XXI.

HOW OUR FREEDOM WAS WON.

"For freedom's battle once begun,
Bequeathed by bleeding sire to son,
Though baffled oft, is ever won." – *Byron*.

XLIV.
Our Freedom is New.

1. NOW I have told you something about the meaning of the word freedom, and how far we in this country are free to do and say what we like without interference. But as I said before, you must not suppose that the freedom which we now enjoy was always possessed by Englishmen.

2. On the contrary, it is because our present liberty has been won for us by our forefathers only by great sacrifices, and has been bought with their fortunes and their lives that we value it so greatly, and are so proud of possessing it. I spoke to you of freedom of thought, and said that a man was free in our country at the present day to think what he chose; but you who have read your English history know only too well that this was not always so.

Freedom of Thought.

3. It was one of the best and purest of Englishmen, Sir Thomas More, who in the reign of Henry VIII was sent to prison, tried, condemned, and at last beheaded because he would not say that he believed the king was the true head of the Church to which he belonged. The king and

those who advised him declared that everyone should take what was called the "Oath of Supremacy"; but More replied, that though he was quite ready to serve the king truly and well, yet that his conscience would not allow him to take the oath in the way the king commanded.

4. But in those days it was not enough that a man should act according to the law, but it was necessary that he should also think that which those who made the law wished him to think. Sir Thomas More was willing enough to obey King Henry, but in his own heart he did not believe that the claim which Henry had made to be head of the Church was a right one.

5. This was an offence which could not be forgiven, and More was sent to the Tower, and after suffering a long and painful imprisonment, was at last beheaded in the year 1535.

6. A very different man from Sir Thomas More was Hugh Latimer, Bishop of Worcester, but in one thing he resembled him. He, too, was put to death because he would not give up the right which all of us nowadays have, of believing what his conscience told him was right.

7. It was in the reign of Queen Mary that Latimer, with another famous bishop, Thomas Ridley, was burnt at Oxford on account of his religion. The words of Latimer as he stood at the stake have become famous: "Be of good comfort, Master Ridley," said he, "and play the man. We shall this day light such a candle, by God's grace, in England, as I trust shall never be put out."

8. Not only did these words prove true, not only did the cause for which Latimer gave up his life grow stronger and prosper through the example of his death, but the cause of freedom of thought in England and throughout the world was helped by the suffering which he and others like him underwent for conscience' sake. For there were many others.

9. It was not More and Latimer alone who gave up their lives rather than deny what they believed to be true; nor was it only for their religious views that Englishmen were persecuted. There have been hundreds and thousands of brave men and women in our history, high and low, rich

and poor, who have stood up for freedom of thought just as truly as the Lord Chancellor and the bishop of whom I have spoken. It is to their courage that we owe our liberty at the present day.

Freedom of the Press.

10. But freedom of thought was not the only freedom which was denied to our forefathers, and which is enjoyed by us.

11. You know in the last chapter I told you something about the liberty of the press which we now enjoy, and I explained to you that as long as we do not injure others by what we write, we who live in this country are free to write and to print what we choose. But this freedom, of which Englishmen are so proud, was for many hundred years denied to them.

12. We who are accustomed as a matter of course to read in a newspaper—which we can buy for a penny—news from every part of the world, may well be astonished to find that only 200 years ago, in the reign of Charles II, the Lord Chief Justice of England, one of the highest judges in the land, declared that by the law of England it was criminal to publish any public news, whether true or false, without the king's leave.

13. And, indeed, when persons were unfortunate enough to offend against the laws by printing what was not permitted, or what was not approved of by those who had power and high position, the punishments which were inflicted upon them were often very severe, and often, too, very unjust.

XLV.
Prynne.

1. In the reign of Charles I, for instance, William Prynne, a lawyer, wrote a book which was displeasing to the king and his friends, and for so doing he was condemned to stand twice in the pillory, and to have his ears cut off. Nor was this cruel treatment thought to

PRYNNE IN THE PILLORY.

be punishment enough. Prynne was fined £5,000, was turned out of his college at the University of Oxford, and was prevented from doing his work as a lawyer.

2. But not even these penalties could shake his determination or compel him to be silent. He wrote another book, and this time it was the Archbishop of Canterbury whom he offended. Again he was put in the pillory, his cheeks were branded with a hot iron, another fine was imposed upon him, and he was thrown into prison. Even then, however, he did not cease writing, and at last his courage met with its reward.

3. His sufferings had won people to his cause, and in the year 1640, he was elected a member of Parliament, and though during the rest of his life he more than once got into further troubles by the boldness of his writing, he did much both by his endurance and by his sufferings to help on the cause of the freedom of the press, for which he had fought so long.

Cobbett.

4. Let me give you another example for which we need not go back nearly so far. It was only in the year 1810, or not a hundred years ago, that William Cobbett, who afterwards became a member of Parliament, was tried and punished for writing things which anybody nowadays could say and write without any interference whatever.

5. He believed that some militiamen had been unfairly punished, and in a paper which belonged to him he spoke of the injustice of the treatment which they had suffered and blamed those who had ordered the punishment. He was brought before the judges, was tried, found guilty, and sentenced to be sent to prison for two years, and to pay a fine of £1,000.

6. So you will see that the freedom of the press which we enjoy was, like freedom of thought, only won by the sufferings of those who lived before our time.

Other Instances.

7. I might give you many more instances of the way in which the freedom we enjoy as a matter of course at the present day has only been won for us bit by bit, by the courage, the suffering, and the determination of those who lived before us.

8. Some of you have, perhaps, been at a great public meeting, and have heard a well-known speaker make a speech to thousands of listeners, about parliament, about an election, or about all sorts of other matters which interest people. No one interferes with such a speaker nowadays, for we have freedom of public meeting. But this was not always so, and over and over again meetings have been broken up by armed men, and both the speakers and the listeners have been imprisoned and punished for daring to take part in such a thing.

9. And so again the freedom to travel where we like and when we like is a new thing. The freedom to buy what we like and to sell what we like, and to get the best price we can for what we sell is a new thing, and there are many other examples. But I think I have said enough to show you how precious a thing is the freedom which we really have, and how terrible it would be to go back to the old state of things where men were punished and persecuted for doing the very things which you and I and all of us do every day, and which we think the commonest and most harmless things in the world.

What we Owe to our Forefathers.

10. It is for these reasons that we need never tire of reading and studying the history of those to whom we owe so much. In the first place, their example is full of encouragement and help to us, for there are many things which we may have to do as citizens of this great country which we shall do better if we imitate the courage and the endurance of those who did so much to make it truly great.

11. And in the second place, we must not forget that the battle which they fought is not really won yet, but that the cause of freedom

A PUBLIC MEETING.

has still to be struggled for in many parts of the world; and indeed the freedom which we have is not after all so sure and so complete that we may not ourselves have some day to give up our best possessions and our lives to keep what we have won even in this country.

CHAPTER XXII.

WATCH-WORDS OF ENGLISH LIBERTY.

"To none will we sell, to none will we deny, to none will we delay,
right and justice."—*Magna Charta.*

XLVI.
Charters and Statutes.

1. THE freedom which we now have, has, as I told you in the last
two chapters, been won by the struggles and sufferings of a great
number of Englishmen at different times in our history and in different ways. Sometimes it has been gained by hard fighting on the
battlefield; at others by eloquent speeches and hard patient work in
Parliament. Some again have been won at last, but only after those
who did most to obtain them had suffered martyrdom and lost their
lives at the stake or on the scaffold.

2. But there is hardly one of our great liberties which has not at
one time or another been made part of the law of the country, and
written down in plain terms, so that no one afterwards would have
any doubt as to what was the real law of the land.

3. It is in the great Charters and in the great Statutes of the
country that these famous laws have usually been written down. The
Charters are the records of the rights which the kings of England
have from time to time granted to the people. The Statutes are the
Acts of Parliament which have been passed by the Lords and Commons, and approved of by the king.

4. I am going, in this chapter, to say something about a few of these written rules upon which so much of our liberty depends.

Magna Charta.

5. Here is one of them, it is nearly the oldest, and perhaps it is the most important.

"No free man shall be taken, or imprisoned, or dispossessed[17], or outlawed, or exiled, or injured in any other way except by the lawful judgment of his peers[18], or by the law of the land."

The meaning of that is plain enough. It means that everybody in the kingdom shall always be entitled to a free and a fair trial, according to law. If indeed this great rule had never been disobeyed, many an unjust and cruel judgment, which has been given at one time or another in our history, would have been avoided. But though our ancestors sometimes fell short of their own laws, still it was always a great thing to have the rule before them to point out what was true justice and wisdom.

Old Laws, Good and Bad.

6. Sometimes you will hear people talk as if laws were bad or useless only because they are old and were made a very long time ago. This is true enough of some laws; those, for instance, which have to do with manners and customs which frequently change. But it is not true of laws which have to do with the great rules of right and wrong, which are as true now as they were 800 years ago, and will be equally true 800 years hence.

7. It is very foolish, therefore, to say that any law is a bad one merely because it is an old one.

8. It is necessary to ask first what the law is before we can say whether it be bad or good. For instance, where do we find this great

17   Turned out of his property.
18   Equals.

KING JOHN SIGNING MAGNA CHARTA.

rule which I told you about just now—this rule which says that "no man shall be judged except by his equals and according to the law of the land." The lawyers would tell you that it is to be found in chapter 9 Henry III.; that is to say, in the ninth chapter of the Statutes passed in the reign of Henry III., and Henry III., as you know, came to the throne in 1216, or 650 years ago.

9. But the way the lawyers put it is not the way we who are not lawyers generally describe it. We say that it is rule thirty-nine of the Great Charter, commonly called "Magna Charta," granted by King John to the Barons of England at Runnymede on behalf of the people of England in the year 1215. And certainly we should be making a great mistake if we called this a bad law just because it is 650 years old.

Another Gift of the Charter.

10. Then there is another great rule in this same Magna Charta which puts into words the true secret of justice, and shows that so long ago as the time of King John, Englishmen knew that in order that the law might be of any real use it should be open to all alike, rich and poor, high and low, and that it should not only be open to everyone to claim his rights through the law, but that everyone should be able to have his claim listened to and attended to immediately, and not be put off from day to day and month to month without justice being done him.

11. In rule forty of the Great Charter you will find these words: -

"To none will we sell, to none will we deny, to none will we delay, right and justice."

Promise and Performance.

12. This is a splendid promise made by the King to the people. If the promise had always been kept by those whose business it was to see justice done, much wrong and much suffering would have been avoided.

13. Unfortunately, there have been many times in our history when judges or magistrates have been found wicked enough to sell their judgments to those who were rich enough to buy them, and have refused them to those who were too poor to do so.

14. There have been times when those who sought justice have been denied it, and because they were weak, or friendless, or disliked, have asked in vain for the rights the law gave them. And lastly, there have been times when those who sought for justice have been put off, and the hearing of their cause has been delayed, until when right was at last done to them it came too late to do them any good. So you will see that despite King John's promise to the Barons, right and justice have been sold, denied, and delayed.

15. But though there have been, and perhaps still may be, cases in which the rule has been broken, yet on the whole it has been a good thing to have it clearly written down for everybody to see and for everybody to appeal to. And the very fact of having such a rule as part of the law of the land has been an advantage, although at times the rule may not have been observed. For though there have been some bad judges, and unjust magistrates in our history, yet on the whole there is no country in the world where the judges have, as a rule, been more upright and honourable, and where justice has been done more regularly and with greater certainty than in our own.

XLVII.
Habeas Corpus.

1. Some of you may perhaps have heard people talk about what is called a "Habeas Corpus." The name is certainly not one which tells us much; it is made up of two Latin words which mean, "Take the body." But though the name is a puzzling one, it has very often been used in our history, for it has to do with one of the great rules of which we have been speaking, by which our freedom is made certain. There was a time, as I have told you, when men and women in this country might be taken to prison without just cause, and kept there for months and sometimes for years without having a fair trial, or indeed any trial.

2. Of course, it was very little use for the law to say, as it did in

Magna Charta, that every man had a right to be tried by his equals. If he were never brought to trial, the rule plainly did not help him at all.

3. Much injustice was done and much suffering was inflicted by the bad and shameful plan of imprisoning men without trial, and many were the complaints that were made against it. It was not, however, till the year 1679, in the reign of King Charles II., that an Act of Parliament was passed which gave a right to every person in the Kingdom to claim a fair trial within a reasonable time, and which did more than that, for it not only gave the right, but what was of still greater importance, it gave a means by which the poorest and most unprotected could insist upon the right being really granted to him.

4. This famous Act of Parliament, which is usually called the Habeas Corpus Act, declares that if any man or woman be imprisoned, whether by the King, or by the order of any court of justice, he or she, or their friends on their behalf, may have what is called a "writ of Habeas Corpus," and which is really an order to the governor of the gaol where the person is imprisoned, or to anyone else who keeps him imprisoned, to bring him before a judge who may determine whether or not his imprisonment be just.

5. Of course, if the law went no further than this, it would be very little use, for there would be no way of making bad judges or magistrates give the order required. But fortunately, there is something more, for the law further says that every judge or magistrate, or other person who has the right to give a writ of Habeas Corpus, must do so, and that if he refuses he shall at once be liable to pay a fine.

6. So that it is not likely that anyone nowadays would be long without the order he wanted.

7. The reason why the words "Habeas Corpus" are used is because they are the first words in the order, which used to be written in Latin. The words, as I told you, mean "You may have the body"; and the order, or writ, commanded the person to whom it was sent to bring

up the "body" or person of the prisoner for trial, so that he might be found guilty or innocent, and punished or released accordingly.

The End of Slavery.

8. In Chapter XII. I told you that no man could be a slave on English soil. It was in the year 1772, in the reign of George III., that a negro slave named Somerset was turned out into the street by his cruel master, because he was ill and unable to work. The slave was found almost dead in the streets by a Mr. Granville Sharp, who, being a kind and humane man, had him taken to the hospital, and found a situation for him when he got well.

9. Two years afterwards, Somerset's old master met him, and at once told a policeman to put him into prison as a runaway slave. "He is my property," said the master, "and no one has any more right to take him away than to take my hat or my coat." Mr. Sharp and the master went to law to settle the dispute, and the Lord Mayor of London, who had to try the case, at once declared that Somerset was free, and that his old master had no right to claim him. But the matter did not end there. The master, in defiance of the Lord Mayor, tried to carry off Somerset again, and at last, the whole matter came before the judges. It was then that Lord Mansfield, speaking on behalf of twelve of the judges, declared that by the law of England a man became free the moment he touched our shores.

10. This great judgment has become another watchword of our freedom, and from the time when it was spoken there would never any longer be a doubt that slavery in England was at an end forever.

The Use of Watchwords.

11. What I want you to understand in all these examples is that, besides gaining a new liberty or a new right, it is always a good thing both for ourselves and for those who come after us that it should be written down clearly in the shape of a law, a charter, the sentence of

a judge, or in some other solemn form, so that not only may there be no uncertainty about it in the future, but that all men may be able ever afterward to refer to the very words themselves and to say—**THAT IS THE LAW.**

The great lesson of this book will be found written very shortly on the slate below

NELSON'S SIGNAL AT THE BATTLE OF TRAFALGAR.

The numbers on the slate were shown by flags hoisted on the mast, by this means the message was conveyed to all the ships in the fleet.

www.ingramcontent.com/pod-product-compliance
Lightning Source LLC
Chambersburg PA
CBHW032003180726
48283CB00008B/2551